This book to be returned on or before the last date below.

1 - NOV 2010

Jane Prowse lives in North London with her film editor husband, Ian, and their two cats, Mitten and blind Buffy. The cats continue to help Jane write by lying on her lap, purring.

Jane's had a great time this year, visiting schools and festivals, giving talks about writing and especially about Hattori Hachi. Work has taken her to the States several times and ninjutsu research has included a trip to Kielder and a whistle-stop tour of Japan.

Hattori Hachi: The Revenge of Praying Mantis was Jane's first book and *Hattori Hachi: Stalking the Enemy* is her second. Jane and the cats are currently working on the third.

HATTORI HACHI

Stalking the Enemy

JANE PROWSE

PICCADILLY PRESS · LONDON

For Mum, who is always there for me.

First published in Great Britain in 2010
by Piccadilly Press Ltd,
5 Castle Road, London NW1 8PR
www.piccadillypress.co.uk

A catalogue record for this book is available
from the British Library

ISBN: 978 1 84812 059 4 (paperback)

1 3 5 7 9 10 8 6 4 2

Printed in the UK by CPI Bookmarque, Croydon, CR0 4TD
Cover design by Patrick Knowles
Cover photo © btrenkel/istockphoto

Mixed Sources
Product group from well-managed
forests and other controlled sources
www.fsc.org   Cert no. TT-COC-002227
© 1996 Forest Stewardship Council
FSC

CHAPTER ONE

'A ninja's roots are buried as deep as the roots of a tree . . .'

If it had been up to me, I'd have told Dad everything. I was tired of pretending and covering up for all the strange activity that had gone on over the last few months. But Mum was adamant.

'Oh Hattie,' she said, one afternoon while the two of us were out on the balcony of our fourth floor flat, bringing in the washing. 'You know your dad – he'll panic. He'll become super-controlling and then neither of us will ever be allowed out of his sight and we'll never find Toby.' I knew she was right. My dad, Ralph, is a community police officer where we live in Camden, North London. He does have a tendency to take charge and do things his own way.

It had been an extraordinary year and, actually, I was finding it hard enough myself to accept everything that had gone on, even though I'd been part of it all. Mum and I had discovered that my twin brother, Toby – who my parents had believed had died in a fire just after we were born – was still alive. It wasn't that Dad would want to hinder us looking for him if he knew the truth, but that he'd turn it into a full-blown police investigation, and we both knew that would never help us defeat the evil ninja warriors who had abducted Mum and who we feared Toby was still involved with.

The whole adventure had started almost a year before when Mum disappeared and I discovered I was from a highly respected, legendary family in Japan. Mum had been kidnapped and I had to train as a ninja warrior to fight the terrifying underground warriors, the Kataki, to rescue her – which I did with the help of my best mates Mad Dog and Neena and my brilliant ninjutsu teacher, Yazuki, who lives on the ground floor of our building.

Things had been relatively normal in the Jackson household since Mum had been home. I'd been revising hard for my GCSEs but I really enjoyed doing all the mundane things with Mum too, like washing and folding sheets. I'd never have thought these tasks could be so precious until I'd had to do them without her all those months. I'd noticed we were spending a lot more time together as a family as well, like going to the zoo or planting tubs on our balcony and even going ice-skating. Dad and I both wanted to keep Mum close to us for fear that she might suddenly disappear again.

In fact, both Mum and I knew it was far more likely to be me who was abducted next time – and probably with no warning at all.

Although I loved having quality time with Mum and Dad, every family activity just made me feel worse about Toby – or Hattori Sarutobi, to call him by his correct ninjutsu name. In Japan, our surnames come first and then our first names last – which is why I'm Hattori Hachi. Hattori was my mum's maiden name and Hachi was my birth name, though I didn't know that either till this time last year.

It was a shock to find out about Toby because I'd never been told I had a twin. And now I'd wake up every night in a sweat, wondering where he was and if he was okay. Mum had told Dad a few things about our ninjutsu history, explaining that her family used to be very important and highly respected in Japan - skilled fighters and sleuths, a bit like James Bond. Dad thought this was great and teased Mum about her being Catwoman or one of Charlie's Angels. But every time I mentioned Toby to Mum and asked whether we should at least tell Dad a bit about him, Mum became very firm.

'When your dad and I were told Toby had died,' she said to me, as we gathered up the last of the washing, 'they brought us his body in a tiny coffin. We had a funeral for him and your father has hardly been able to speak about him since.' She paused, looking out over the wasteland at the back of our flat and the London skyline beyond. I could see the memory of the fire was still extremely painful for Mum, even though she knew Toby hadn't died but had been stolen. She looked back at me. 'Your dad blames himself for not being able to get inside the burning building to save him.'

'But it wasn't Toby inside that coffin, Dad needs to know that —'

'Yes, but telling your dad he was deceived will bring up all kinds of emotions for him, some of them not at all pleasant – especially when he realises Toby was here so often last year, right under his nose. He may even simply refuse to believe he's his son. We have to know Toby's okay and that he wants to come back into our lives before I'd even consider putting your father through all that.'

We went inside and Mum glanced at the clock. '*Tempus fugit*,' she said. 'I don't know where the hours go. Pass me my shoes will you?' Even though Mum was only heading across the wasteland to The Foundry to give a reading class at the children's home she'd helped set up, I felt a pang of unease. This was partly because she was putting on her split-toed socks, which was a sign she was preparing for action. Our ninjutsu clothes included split-toed canvas shoes, *tabi*, that give a better grip for balancing and hiding in trees – which is why we had to wear these strange socks. Mum saw me looking at her.

'Need to get some new ones of these,' she said, smiling. One of her socks had a big hole in the heel.

'Wear mine,' I said, and handed her the ones my best friend Neena had given me for a joke. They were black with the split toe, just like Mum's, but Neena had embroidered *Work Socks* in silver thread on the ankle. It was Neena's way of reminding me that ninjutsu wasn't everything in life. She loves shopping and she's always trying to persuade me to buy short skirts and high heels and to wear girly clothes

4

instead of my usual black trousers, T-shirt, and flat shoes that kept me prepared for any ninjutsu activity.

Mum put on my socks and her trainers and grabbed her bag, checking she had her canvas *tabi* shoes and ninjutsu hood.

'Love you, sweetheart,' she said. 'Now go and revise!'

'Love you too, Mum,' I shouted back, and with that she was gone.

Even though I was working hard for my exams, there was always ninja work to be done. That's how Yazuki came to be chatting to me and Neena in my bedroom at four o'clock that afternoon, curtains drawn, after Mum had gone out and Dad was sleeping before doing a night shift at work. Neena had her back to me and Yazuki was messing around, putting some make-up on her while I desperately tried to cram some GCSE geography revision.

'The Kataki are well hidden – and plotting,' Yazuki announced. 'They seek to control the Golden Child, the only one who can help them fulfil their plans. Whatever we can do to protect you, Hattie, we must. They will be looking for you, especially as your sixteenth birthday approaches.' When I was sixteen, I'd be able to sign the ancient scroll that would make me the Hattori Golden Child, heir to the family wealth and power, and so I would be far more valuable to the Kataki. 'Any small act that confuses the enemy and buys you some time could be critical,' Yazuki continued. 'So, since you and Neena spend so much time together, I'd like you to swap clothes whenever you're out, even if it's just a coat or a hat.'

I laughed out loud as Neena looked at me, aghast.

'Really?' asked Neena.

I knew what Neena was thinking: she wouldn't be seen dead in any of my clothes, especially not the ninja ones. Neena's half Trinidadian and bright colours really suit her. She loves anything fluorescent or patterned and spends hours and hours shopping and getting dressed. And she has a real weakness for high-heeled shoes.

'I'm sure you agree Hattie's life is more important than fashion,' Yazuki said.

'*As* important, maybe . . .' said Neena hopefully. 'No, I'm kidding. Of course I'll wear Hattie's clothes, but maybe I could at least take her shopping first?'

In the past, Yazuki had always argued that disguise and deception relied on changing your body shape and tricking the enemy's eye. But ever since Mum came home, Yazuki had been hatching plans for how to trick the enemy in every possible way. The previous day she'd spent a whole hour taking an imprint of my face, for reasons she wouldn't reveal. With my birthday coming up and the whole Golden Child issue looming, we all knew that the Kataki pressure could suddenly intensify and Yazuki wanted to be prepared.

'Only five days till your birthday, Hattie,' said Neena, leafing through a recipe book she'd taken from my shelf.

'Sit still, Neena, please,' Yazuki said, make-up sponge in hand. 'Just for a second.'

'Will we have a scroll-signing ceremony or something?' Neena continued. 'I mean, should I be making some kind of special cake or can we have Death by Chocolate or cheesecake for Hattie's birthday like we usually do?'

'There will be no special occasion regarding the scroll,' Yazuki answered. 'Hattie will sign at midnight as she goes into the day of her sixteenth birthday, as is traditional when inheriting any kind of ninjutsu title, and then life will continue as normal and nothing will be mentioned or acted upon regarding her new role as the Hattori Golden Child. At least, not until her exams are over.'

'What about everything she'll inherit in Japan? Will you all be going?' Neena asked. 'Can I come?'

'Stop wriggling, Neena,' Yazuki grumbled, 'or you won't be going anywhere.'

The scroll was a very, very old document that had been drafted almost a thousand years ago and gave special wealth, power and privileges to the person who inherited it on their sixteenth birthday, when they would become the Hattori 'Golden Child'. Yazuki had discovered the Golden Child status only came around every seventh generation. The hope was that peace could be achieved in the intervening decades – but if there was ongoing feuding, the Golden Child had the power to bring an end to any fighting. As far as we understood, our extended family was definitely not at peace. The Kataki battles had started many years ago, but we still had no idea why. If I was to inherit the title, it would be up to me to stop all the fighting. So no pressure there then . . .

We all knew Toby had just as much right to the Golden Child status as me. According to legend and the scroll itself, when twins are born, whichever is in possession of the scroll and signs it on the day of their sixteenth birthday will become the Golden Child. Which is why Yazuki had it locked away in her safe.

'It all seems terribly complicated,' Neena said. 'What would happen if either Hattie or Toby died before their birthday?'

'Thanks for that happy thought,' I said.

'Nothing in old ninja law is simple,' Yazuki replied. 'If either twin dies, the title passes to the other. But if the scroll is not signed on the actual day of their sixteenth birthday, then the Golden Child status defers for another seven generations.'

'So what is it the Hattoris have, exactly,' Neena asked, 'that's going to make this Golden Child so powerful?'

'It's what they don't have yet,' Yazuki answered. 'A weapon so terrifying it could cause global devastation if it gets into the wrong hands. However, it's nothing we need to worry about today.'

'Who was the last Golden Child, seven generations ago then?' I asked. 'Anyone important?'

'Hattori Junpei,' Yazuki replied, tight-lipped. 'Nearly two hundred years ago. He was your great, great, great, great, great-grandfather and he was where the trouble started. He was unable to keep the peace.'

'What happened to him?' I'd never been told anything about my mum's ancestors.

'He died a natural death while the families feuded around him. I have no more to say about him, since I don't wish to speak ill of the dead. We cannot let Toby sign the scroll if he's one of the Kataki – that would entitle him to the Hattori weapon, power and wealth. Their organisation will become a rallying point for warriors from all over the world. We have no idea whether Toby is a friend to us or not, and since we already have first-hand experience of how brutal even a family member can be —'

She carried on talking but I didn't hear another word. My chest felt like a vice had gripped me as terror consumed me and my mind was suddenly ablaze with images from the mind-merge I'd had with my Aunt Suzi, who had turned out to be our worst enemy, Praying Mantis, the person who had abducted Mum. I had managed to defeat Suzi in a terrifying battle, but in the process had experienced a kind of melting together of our brains where I was overcome with sounds and images: a hospital . . . me, a tiny baby . . . the darkest, blackest mood engulfing me, the sound of screaming inside my head, flames all around, the terrible stench of burning – a raven swooping past with huge, flapping wings . . . This mind-merge had haunted me ever since I'd fought my Aunt Suzi. She was Mum's step-sister and had been so jealous of Mum she'd stolen Toby just days after he was born, hoping to use him to inherit this very title we were talking about. As fast as the vision came, it dispersed – leaving me shaking and riddled with guilt.

'It could have been me that was taken,' I said. This thought had consumed me daily. I'd talked at length to Mum, Yazuki and Neena, but no one had been able to make me feel better. Yazuki wasn't about to have the conversation again.

'Okay, we're done,' Yazuki said. 'What do you think, Hattie?' I looked up, still dazed, and experienced the strangest sensation I'd ever felt in my life.

In the mirror there were three Hattie Jacksons, all identical. Me, Neena and Yazuki – the two of them wearing latex face masks with long dark hair, exactly matching mine, and me with my mouth half open, just staring back at them.

Neena started giggling. 'Oh Hattie,' she said, 'I've always wanted to look like you and now I do! It's INCREDIBLE!' She leapt to her feet, checking herself out in the full-length mirror. 'Never going to have your figure though, am I?'

'Near enough,' Yazuki said. 'Put on the jacket.'

Neena put on my shimmering dark bluey-black ninja jacket over her bright pink top and, although it was pretty tight, it was enough to fool anyone in the semi-darkness. She kicked out a leg, as though to strike an opponent, then yelled in pain. 'Okay, so I won't try any of the moves,' she said.

There was a shuffling noise on the balcony and a tap on the window.

'Hattie, you there?' came a cheerful voice.

'Mad Dog!' Neena whispered. 'See if he can tell the difference!'

'No!' said Yazuki. 'There's no need for him to know about these disguises. *Only tell a ninja what each ninja needs to know.* If he is aware we have this deception at our fingertips, he may one day fail Hattie, thinking it's one of us, dressed as her. The disguise will only work if everyone

– friend and enemy – believes the imposter is Hattie.'

'But I tell Mad Dog everything,' I said.

Yazuki turned to look at me, her eyes boring into mine. I could tell she wanted to discuss something with me before I went anywhere, so I called out to Mad Dog.

'Down later!'

Yazuki waited till we heard him climb back over the balcony and make his way down the rope we'd recently installed. 'Are you involved with him?' she asked.

'What? No. Well, yes, maybe. Just as a friend,' I muttered, knowing I was blushing. I looked down, pretending to suddenly be engrossed in learning about the rivers of North-East England.

'Hattie, I need to know exactly what your relationship is if I'm to leave him in charge of you – emotional entanglement will affect his ability to make rational decisions.'

'In charge? Why? Where are you going?' I said, looking up again.

'It's usual for teenage girls to lie about their flirtations but not you, Hattie. You must tell the truth. Are you romantically involved with Mad Dog?'

Two pairs of eyes were burning into me now – both from faces that looked exactly like mine. The afternoon was definitely getting stranger by the minute.

'Well, I do like him. I like him a lot, but I don't . . . we don't . . .' I trailed off. The truth was, I didn't know how I felt about Mad Dog. He was absolutely certain how he felt about me though. He'd already told Neena he'd marry me tomorrow if he could, but I was a million miles from even going out with him at the moment and he knew it. The only thing on my mind was getting through my exams, then finding Toby so we could bring him home. Besides, I couldn't risk complicating things with Mad Dog as I relied on him to do my ninjutsu training with me. 'I don't want Mad Dog telling me what to do,' was all I said.

'I'm pretty impressed with him, I have to say,' said Neena. 'Now his lovely blond hair's grown back and covered up the tattoo on his head, he's really fit. He's got gorgeous green eyes as well. I even saw Tasha Weaver eyeing him up the other day.' Neena always teased me about Tasha Weaver who lived over the road, trying to make me think she was after Mad Dog so I'd admit I had feelings for him. I refused to be drawn.

'He wants to look after me, that's all. And we're not romantically involved. We're both aware emotional attachments can cause a ninja to make mistakes.'

Yazuki narrowed her eyes like she always did when she was grilling me. 'I won't always be here for you, Hattie,' she said. 'That's a fact you must face. Sometimes I receive ninjutsu orders of my own.'

My heart started pounding. I'd been so happy things had been back to normal, at least for a few weeks. I couldn't bear the idea all that it was about to change again. 'Are you going somewhere? Please, you have to tell me.'

'Look at the time!' Yazuki suddenly said, rushing back into the living room. 'I have laundry to deliver!' She grabbed her things and dashed to the door, just pausing to say, 'Keep focused on the matter in hand, Hattie Jackson. Revision!'

CHAPTER TWO

'Say nothing until your words have meaning.'

It was getting late when Neena went back to her place, leaving me with a pile of notes and some energy bars to keep me going. I'd hardly picked up the first page of maths revision when there was another tap on my bedroom window.

'Hattie! How long are you going to be? Come and practise – exercise is good for brain power.' I couldn't put Mad Dog off any longer, so I went down to Yazuki's 'dojo' – the home of our ninjutsu training. It was a lovely, airy room in her semi-basement that had a glass wall and sliding door leading into her Zen garden at the back. It had a light wood floor and all kinds of ninjutsu tools and weapons on the walls, as well as springboards and a giant Buddha with long earlobes keeping an eye on us all.

As I walked into the room I had to laugh. Even though all the Foundry kids who had been caught up in our last adventure had now moved back to the children's home, Mad Dog had got them round to form a mini Kataki army to see if I could still fight a group of attackers and win. None of them had any idea to this day what had really gone on in the disused underground tunnels beneath the Foundry, all those months when they'd been kept prisoner by Praying Mantis – and Mr Bell who ran the Leisure Centre. They believed Mr Bell was just some weird psycho who had a crazy plan for taking over the world, but who then died when he fell into the canal, drunk, the night Mum escaped and they were rescued as well. They had no idea Mr Bell had also been a Kataki infiltrator.

Since the Foundry kids had found out we had a dojo, they'd all been really keen to learn ninjutsu. They each had an animus – the spirit of a creature that determines how you behave in battle and always means you cast that creature's shadow when you're fighting. Mine was a cat, just like Mum's. Mad Dog was a spider, and in front of me now were all kinds of shadows – a puppy, a kitten, a baby gorilla, as well as a little snake and a couple of strange-looking insects.

Even though there were seven of them, it was no contest. Instinctively, I grabbed a metre-long *hambo* stick, ran across the wooden floor, ducking, parrying, striking and blocking their attacks, and laid all seven kids straight out on the ground. I didn't hurt them – they'd been trained to give in before an opponent did them any damage. They knew I'd been blessed with almost superhuman fighting skills, partly inherited from my ninjutsu family in Japan and partly developed through all those months of intensive training. In fact, I'd been preparing for this my whole life, although I'd never realised it – Mum had been training me in ninja techniques since I was a baby.

As I held my *hambo* triumphantly above my head, I even got a round of applause. Mad Dog was the only one still on his feet: he and I never fought each other in front of the Foundry kids. For a start it could look pretty scary – as though he really was trying to kill me. And besides, we didn't want to give away any of our well-rehearsed techniques because, even though I trusted these kids, I could never know for sure who might be spying for the Kataki.

Everything felt relatively normal and happy . . . So why was I feeling so weird? Yazuki was out delivering laundry to various clients. Dad would soon be out, happy as anything to be back on his community police officer rounds and Mum was over at the Foundry giving reading lessons to some of the younger children. Or was she? Out of nowhere, I had a blinding vision that she wasn't – that something was going on and things weren't right.

Panic overwhelmed me. I was in the middle of doing another of my party pieces for the kids – walking on the ceiling dangling upside down, thanks to my extra strong climbing claws – but in my panic I nearly slipped. I dropped down, leaving my climbing claws still stuck into the ceiling and, without telling the others what I was doing, I legged it out of the dojo and over the back wall and ran full pelt across the wasteland to the Foundry.

When I got there, Mum was sitting quietly in the big,

cosy kitchen with three of the youngest children at a table piled with books. She smiled, pleased as ever to see me.

'Hi Hattie. Having trouble with your revision?' she asked, pulling a chair out for me to sit down.

'Hi, no, well yes – no, are you okay?'

'What is it? What's up?' she said as Mad Dog came running in, only seconds behind me.

'Something's not right, Mum. I thought it was you, but maybe it's Yazuki . . .' Part of my ninjutsu training was to develop my already sensitive psychic skills. It was part of the highest level of training – the Fifth Dan – that I'd passed before I went off to rescue Mum. It was a mental state called *ku*, where I could drop into a semi-trance and pick up things instinctively, sometimes even predicting what someone was going to do. This skill of mine was getting stronger by the day. Sometimes it was a blessing but mostly it still scared and confused me.

Mad Dog put on the kettle and nodded to the Foundry kids. 'Okay, outside, you lot. Go and play for a while.' They were out of the door like a shot. Mad Dog sat down, serious, at the table. 'I think you should tell her, Chiyoko,' he said. It slightly irritated me that he acted all adult and used Mum's first name, especially since he was discussing something to do with me.

'Tell me what?' I asked.

Mum smiled again. 'There *is* something going on that you might have sensed. I'm going to Kielder with Yazuki to look for Toby and, before you even ask, no, you can't come. I know you can't bear me being out of your sight even for a few hours and I know you want to find Toby more than anything, but you have to stay here, Hattie – to finish your exams for one thing, but more importantly, to stay away from the people who want to kill you.'

'But —'

'But nothing. I was thinking about just taking off with Yazuki tonight while you were asleep,' she said. 'But Mad Dog helped convince me that would be even more upsetting for you. But I *am* going and you *are* staying and that's the end of any discussion about it.'

'Has something happened up there?' I asked, knowing Kielder was the Kataki's headquarters. This bit of information had obsessed me over the weeks. I'd spent hours reading about the area in Northumberland, particularly when I found out it was also where my dad was born. It seemed such a coincidence, but Mum didn't know of any reason why Dad and the Kataki would be connected. She thought the Kataki had made a base up there because the area was so sparsely populated and there were hundreds of acres of forest where it would be easy for them to gather and train without anyone knowing.

'I know nothing more than that I have received instructions to go,' she said.

'Who from?'

'My *chunin* – and that's all I'm going to tell you for now,' she said. Mum didn't want to tell me anything new about ninjutsu while I was revising. Perhaps she thought it would clog up my brain or something. I made a mental note to research *chunin* as soon as I could.

'I don't like you going off without me. And neither will Dad.'

'As far as your dad's concerned, I'm just taking Yazuki to visit her Chinese medicine friend. As I said, Hattie, there's nothing to worry about and we'll be back before you know it.'

I could tell Mum wasn't in the mood to argue, so I just nodded. *Get out of this situation,* I thought to myself. *Don't make any promises you can't keep, then work out with Mad Dog how you're going to talk your way into a trip to Kielder . . .*

I don't know why I bothered thinking I could make plans – nothing ever works out how I expect it to. Mad Dog and I hadn't even stepped into the dojo before we realised something was seriously wrong. Nothing was out of place, no one was there to greet us – but one small detail was different. The door to Yazuki's special cupboard was ajar. No one went in that cupboard without Yazuki's permission – and her van wasn't outside, so I felt sure she wasn't back yet. I glanced at Mad Dog. For a moment, neither of us moved, not sure if the person who'd opened the cupboard was still around. Silently, I took a long Samurai sword off the wall. I reached out to pull the door wide open so we could see inside. Yazuki kept a small safe in there, which she never opened with anyone else around. The safe was open – and it was empty.

The Golden Child scroll had gone.

My heart leapt up into my mouth. All we had to do was to hold on to that scroll until my sixteenth birthday! We all knew the Kataki would be after it. Why had we left the place unguarded, even for a few minutes?

'Why didn't you lock up the dojo?' I said to Mad Dog, barely able to speak.

'I did,' he replied softly, 'right after I'd got all the Foundry kids out.'

A voice came from behind and we both swung round. It was Yazuki.

'Hattie, the scroll disappearing has nothing to do with you. Don't waste energy wondering how or why or who. Focus on your task in hand and let others do what they have to do. Your mum has made arrangements for you to stay here with your dad. He knows we're going to Kielder to visit my Chinese medicine friend, who he believes is ill and needs my help,' she said, already changing into her ninja clothes. 'We're leaving now and I have no idea when we'll be back so don't even ask for any more details.' She moved so fast that she'd already got her everyday clothes on top of her ninja outfit. 'You must not try to follow or contact us or do anything other than finish your exams. Mad Dog – move up to the Jacksons' living room to sleep, as Hattie's dad is on a night shift. Protect Hattie and don't distract her from her revision.'

'No problemo.' Mad Dog beamed, delighted with the instruction that meant he'd be sleeping in our flat tonight.

'Hattie,' Yazuki said, turning to bore holes in me with her intense eyes, 'remember our discussion earlier. Do not let your heart confuse your mind. Keep strictly to the instructions I have given you about focusing on work and not letting your emotions run away with you.' Yazuki needn't have worried – nothing could have been further from my mind than a romantic evening with Mad Dog while Yazuki and Mum were heading into the heart of Kataki training territory.

With that, Yazuki flew out of the door and was gone. I knew she'd pick Mum up on the way and any plans I may have had about convincing them to let me go with them to Kielder were now very firmly out of the window.

Mad Dog locked up the dojo and came with me upstairs, carrying all his bedding so he could sleep on the sofa. He carefully bolted the front door to our flat and checked to make sure the window locks were secure.

'Too late now for revision, surely?' he said, putting some popcorn in the microwave. 'Pick a DVD – anything you like.' We both loved any kind of martial arts film as we were always looking for new ideas for fighting. But I wasn't in the mood. Worrying about the scroll had set me off thinking about my Aunt Suzi all over again – and the raven that had flown at me in my mind-merge with her. I wanted to go online and do some family research.

'You know you're going to have to calm down about Suzi sooner or later,' Mad Dog said, knowing what my family research always honed in on. 'Yazuki checks all the time – your dear Aunt Suzi, Praying Mantis, is still safely behind bars in Japan.'

'It's not her I'm worried about,' I told him. 'It's this terrifying bird I keep seeing in my head. It was so huge, I feel sure it was more likely a person – when I merged minds with Suzi, I was overwhelmed by the terror she feels in its presence.'

Mad Dog knew how to calm me when I got like this, fretting and pacing and unable to concentrate on school-work or relaxing or anything else. He always started with some simple ninja exercise, one of the ones we'd learnt in our first level of training, the First Dan, which was about hand-to-hand combat and knowing when to run rather than fight. He began an exercise where we just mirrored each other's actions, then he progressed into fighting routines, using ninjutsu as though we were almost dancing, moving slowly and gracefully round, anticipating each other's every move. On any other evening, I'd have been two steps ahead of him, but with Mum gone to Kielder and me about as tense as I could be worrying about her, it wasn't long before he caught my arm, twisted my body, grabbed each of my hands in his from behind and forced me to my knees in a well-known ninja hold called *ryoyokudori*, or 'catching both wings'. He reached under my arms, pulling my shoulders back to stop me from moving anywhere.

'You win!' I said, but he didn't let go. He just buried his face in my neck and hugged me in this weird fighting pose. The lamp was throwing our shadows on to the wall and, for once, we weren't cat and spider, our ninja animus shapes, but just Mad Dog and Hattie Jackson, perilously close to kissing. My heart fluttered and for a second I thought, '*If only . . .*' But then Yazuki's warning voice rang out in my mind and I knew this was no time for confusing my emotions. Out of nowhere, I somersaulted forward, pulling Mad Dog off balance and twisting his arms as I got to my feet. He yelled – more with shock than in pain

– as I laughed and said, 'In that hold, the victim's fingers have to be bent right back or it just doesn't work.' I kissed his forehead as he knelt on the floor looking mildly hurt. 'Goodnight Mad Dog and thanks for being . . . well, the best. At everything. Couldn't manage without you,' I said.

I went to bed, leaving Mad Dog grinning as he took his post on guard outside my bedroom door. I knew he wouldn't sleep, taking his role as my protector very seriously indeed.

A nightmare woke me – I was sweating, even though it wasn't hot. It was chemistry revision all mixed up with ninja warriors wielding sabres the size of elephant tusks and a monstrous bird-man swooping down on me trying to peck out my eyes while Mum said over and over, *Why did you tell them the code?*

As far as I knew, only four people had the code to Yazuki's safe – me, Mum, Yazuki and Mad Dog. No wonder I felt so disturbed.

It was still quite early in the morning, but moments later I heard a noise in the living room and a gentle tap on my bedroom door.

'Are you awake?' he whispered. 'Sounded like you were having a nightmare.'

'I'm fine. Come in,' I said, sitting up and smoothing my covers so I looked halfway decent.

Mad Dog shut the door behind him. 'I hope your mum and Yazuki don't think I was dumb enough to tell someone how to get into the safe,' he blurted.

'Did you?' I asked.

'Hattie! What do you take me for?'

'Just had to ask,' I said. 'So who did?'

'No idea.' That's as far as we got with our super-detection work because my phone buzzed with a text from Neena. *R u up? Coming over. Drill started and head about 2 explode.*

They were digging up the road outside Neena's house, which is why she was doing most of her revision at my place.

I texted back: *B quick – things kicking off again!* We'd given Neena a key as she was coming over so often to revise. I heard her letting herself in on the ground floor before I'd even finished getting showered and dressed. She came bounding up the stairs two at a time, laden with books and a bag of clothes. Her mum and dad had agreed she could stay with me for the next few days while they went off to a wedding. We both had nearly a week to revise before our next exam and we didn't have to go to school except to sit the papers, so she was staying right up until my birthday on Tuesday.

'What news then?' Neena grinned – much more excited than I was about the possibility of new Kataki activity. She threw down her bag and started getting breakfast ready for all of us. She'd brought some strange things she'd picked up from the market and some other ingredients I wasn't sure how she'd come by.

'Scroll's gone,' I told her, 'Mum and Yazuki have gone to Kielder, I'm having nightmares and I think I'm going to throw up.'

'But she's not leaving the building,' Mad Dog added, smiling like he ruled my life these days.

23

'Says who?!' I snapped back at him. For a while, no one said anything. Neena fed us delicious patties – some kind of kale or spinach and tasty seasoning, which she said had powerful properties to help my brain. I have to say I was impressed by her commitment to my ongoing ninja mental state.

While we ate, Mad Dog filled her in.

'Hattie,' Neena eventually said, 'I think Mad Dog's right and you should do what your mum and Yazuki told you. They'll probably be back before you know it and anyway, what can you possibly do if you don't know where they are or what they're up to? Oh – this was in your letterbox downstairs.'

She handed me a plain white envelope with my name and address written all in capital letters. Inside, was a faded old postcard with some faint writing on the back. It had five words written across the top. *Act quick – time running out.*

My heart stopped. I turned the postcard over and looked at the picture. It was a very old photo of a small village and had *Kielder* printed along the bottom. The envelope had a Kielder postmark as well. I looked back at the writing – then at what was written below it.

T
D
D
T

wage war
Tanil

I looked at it blankly, then at Neena, then at Mad Dog. 'Okay, so now what do I do?' I said.

I heard the front door again and Dad flew up the stairs. He let himself into our flat and was relieved to see I was already awake.

'Did you hear from your mum?' he asked.

'Not since she left with Yazuki.'

'I'm not at all happy,' he groaned, sinking on to the sofa. 'Hello Neena, hi Mad Dog,' he added. 'Sorry you guys, don't let me interrupt your breakfast.' He got out his mobile and starting dialling. He tried the same number over and over and I knew he was trying to get hold of Mum.

'Probably a bit of a black hole up there for mobiles,' I said.

'Yes, you may be right,' he muttered. 'It's been on answerphone all night.'

'You okay, Dad?'

'Sure, sure, no problem,' he said, jumping to his feet. 'Why would she just go off without discussing it with me? After all we've been through?'

I glanced at Mad Dog and Neena for help. I was slightly lost for words as I hadn't wanted Mum to go off and leave us either.

'Apparently Yazuki's friend's not well,' Mad Dog told him.

'I could have driven them. It's my long weekend off now – I'd have loved to go up to Kielder. I was born there, you know.'

I didn't even stop to think. 'Yes,' I blurted out, 'funny you should mention that. I've got to finish some coursework on family trees for general studies. I missed the whole project and I don't have any information at all about your family or Mum's.'

Neena just looked at me, wide-eyed. I heard Mad Dog mutter, almost inaudibly, 'Hattie, stop . . .'

But I couldn't help myself. 'What would help me most of all in the whole world,' I said to Dad, pouring him a cup of coffee and giving him my best sweet, helpless look, 'would be if you could tell me some things about your side of the family. Milk?'

It took no time at all to persuade Dad that I was going stir-crazy, cooped up in our flat, and that the best way for me to revise was for Dad to drive me, Neena and Mad Dog to Kielder for a first-hand look at some of his family history. To say he leapt at the chance would be an understatement.

'It's the universe telling us it's time for me to go back to revisit my roots,' he said. Even with Mad Dog and Neena protesting, Dad got the map out, already making plans about how Neena and I could revise in the car, while Mad Dog studied the area so he'd be able to take us girls for some long walks in Kielder forest to clear our brains while Dad did some research at Newcastle library about his side of the family. This way, he reasoned, I would get top marks for my brilliance in researching my genealogy and get A stars for all my other subjects as well, because of the time I'd have with Neena with nothing to focus on except revision.

I got straight on to the internet to find somewhere to

stay and chose a lovely little bed and breakfast on the edge of Kielder forest. Mad Dog popped over to Tasha Weaver's Mum's pizza place across the road to pick up some food for the journey, then put a sign on the laundry window – *Closed for stocktaking* – figuring that Yazuki's wrath at the lost laundry takings had to be better than me going to Kielder without him. Neena rang her mum and dad and asked if it was okay for her to go away with Dad and me for a few of days. They couldn't have been more delighted, knowing that fresh air would be good for Neena and that she was so hard-working she'd never stop revising, even if she was on the move.

In less than an hour, our bags were in the car and we were on the road.

CHAPTER THREE

'Know the unknowable . . .'

Dad whistled all the way to Newcastle. It was his 'thinking' whistle, which he did whenever he had something on his mind. I knew he was in the same mental place as me – anxious to get to Kielder so we'd be nearer to Mum, and hugely relieved that he was actively doing something positive, rather than sitting at home worrying about her. He and Mum were even closer these days than they had been before Mum went missing, which is saying something. Everyone said they had the perfect marriage. Dad said it was openness and honesty that made them so compatible. I often wondered how he'd react when he found out just how many secrets Mum had been keeping from him over the years and especially over the last few weeks.

Mad Dog sat in the front while Neena and I crammed our chemistry in the back. She sat behind Mad Dog and I was behind Dad and although I desperately wanted to improve my scant chemistry knowledge, I was far more interested in watching Mad Dog trying to get to know Dad better and wanting to impress him. It was hilarious. They talked about everything to do with the police and the Foundry and what's wrong with kids today. It was heart-warming that Dad had stopped treating Mad Dog like a criminal – quite the opposite, in fact. He was something of Dad's hero, now Dad thought Mad Dog had helped keep Mum alive all those months that she was imprisoned underground in London's disused tube tunnels. Of course, Dad didn't exactly know the truth of that situation either – that after a while we'd known she was down there but hadn't told him. But I was happy for him to be misinformed if it meant he was going to carry on being this nice to Mad Dog.

'I've always respected the police force,' Mad Dog said. 'It's a tough job and a lot of kids I know wouldn't do it, even though they pretend they're hard ...' Mad Dog looked round and caught me watching him. He winked and I blushed.

'Thought you said the police were a bunch of criminals who shouldn't be allowed on the streets,' I teased. 'Only joking, Dad. We all love you really.'

'And what do you think can be done to help these hard-nosed street kids?' Dad asked Mad Dog.

'Take them seriously, give them a home, an education – the kind of things your wonderful wife is doing, actually,' Mad Dog said, in his thoughtful, serious voice.

I smiled to myself, thinking how much Mad Dog had changed over the last year. He was so much more confident now. When Mad Dog's questions dried up, I fed him lines, scribbled on pieces of paper carried to him by my pet ninja rats, Bushi and Akira. Things like, *Tell me about your police training, Mr Jackson* and, *But let's look at it the other way – what can the youth of today do to help the police?*

Neena ignored all of us, her nose buried deep in revision. She took schoolwork really seriously. I did some revising as well, but also used the journey to train Bushi and Akira in a new ninja skill – stealing Mad Dog's keys from his pocket and bringing them to me. He didn't feel a thing and they each got a tiny piece of cheese from my pocket as a reward.

It was a five and a half hour drive up the A1. We stopped once, about halfway there at Ferrybridge Services for a loo break and some drinks to go with our cold pizza, but otherwise we kept on motoring. Bushi curled up to sleep in my pocket, just like she always did, while Akira went to sleep inside Mad Dog's fleece. Mad Dog always wore the same type of clothes these days – black jogging pants, black trainers and a black fleece that had loads of pockets where he could keep useful ninja tools such as string, throwing stars and other small weapons. He hadn't got very far with his official training yet and, although he had earned a ninjutsu jacket of his own, he felt less conspicuous in his own dark street clothes. In one of the pockets in his fleece he'd made a special sleeping place for Akira. Mad Dog was always worried he'd accidentally squash the rats when they were hiding on him, but I knew that both Bushi and Akira were much smarter than that. They could move around really fast inside your clothes, as though they could anticipate your moves. But Mad Dog had made a tough leather pouch about the size of a fizzy drinks can. It was open at one end and, although it was a tight squeeze, there was just enough room for one rat to curl up asleep in it, with no fear of being flattened.

The weather got colder as we travelled north and by the time we got to Durham, it felt more like November than June. I was very glad I'd brought a warm jacket – my favourite dark blue one with a big hood. A little while later, we drove past the *Angel of the North* – the wonderful sculpture of a massive human figure with enormous wings, and Dad decided it was time to start making firm plans.

'Newcastle library first then?' he asked, 'or straight to Kielder to check in to the bed and breakfast?'

'Kielder,' Mad Dog, Neena and I all said at once, knowing that none of us really wanted to go to the library to research my family tree. Dad happily skirted round Newcastle and headed further north towards Morpeth. I'd seen all these names on maps that I'd studied, looking for clues about the Kataki and why they'd be congregating in Kielder. As we got to the Upper North Tyne Valley in Northumberland, the landscape changed and the houses got fewer and further apart. At this altitude there wasn't much farming – there was just a lot of forest and sheep up here on the moors.

'It's strange I've never been to where you were born before, Dad,' I said.

'It was never the right time, was it?' he mumbled. But it *was* strange because we'd travelled so much of the country in my life, moving home every few years – and we'd even spent a few months living in Cumbria, less than an hour away from Kielder. But Dad always avoided going back to visit. I thought it was because his parents were both killed there in a car crash when he was only seven. It seemed to me like he'd locked away all the agony of losing them and he was frightened that if he came back it might just overwhelm him. I understood – I'd had a pretty big dose of those feelings myself all the time Mum had been missing. But now it was different. Mum was here somewhere, so it was the only place in the world either of us wanted to be.

We'd both left her several messages now. I was sure she'd be upset with me for blatantly ignoring her orders to stay at home and revise, but she didn't know about the postcard calling me to Kielder. In my mind, that overruled anything she and Yazuki had told me because, at the very least, I had to find them and tell them about it.

By the time we arrived at the edge of Kielder forest, nearly forty miles north of Newcastle, the weather was really closing in. It was drizzling and there was a thin mist coming down across the rolling hills that led to the border with the Scottish Highlands. I'd read that low cloud could descend at a moment's notice and that mist rose from the reservoir at Kielder all year round because it was such a massive body of water. My sense of foreboding returned – but I wasn't going to let Dad know. He just got more animated, the closer we got.

'Can you believe I haven't been back in about . . . oh . . .

must be thirty-five years? Hasn't changed a bit! I wondered how he could tell whether a clump or two of trees had changed or not. 'Oh that's where my granddad took me on my first fishing trip!' Dad continued enthusiastically, as we passed a stream meandering its way towards the river Tyne.

I guessed he wasn't really feeling as enthusiastic as he made out, but was pretending so that none of us would see how uneasy he really felt. I knew we had to get rid of him as soon as possible, or his trip down memory lane might take up the whole weekend and we needed some time by ourselves to work out how we were going to find Mum and Yazuki. But then suddenly Dad went quiet. We were on a country lane, heading for a level crossing. He stopped just short of it and got out of the car. He just stood there and his eyes started welling up with tears. This must have been the level crossing where his parents' car was hit. The three of us sat in silence in the car, not saying a word. I knew it was grief overwhelming him and I felt sad I couldn't make him feel better. It broke my heart to see him suffer. Even Bushi and Akira sensed the atmosphere. Bushi poked her nose out of my pocket and twitched her whiskers at me as Akira scampered back from Mad Dog and climbed into my pocket beside her. It seemed like ages that we all sat there, then eventually Dad blew his nose and got back in the car.

'Just listen out for the tolling bell,' he said. 'It's a ghostly, haunting, watery sound which legend says is a warning sign of impending agony, even death. If you hear it, you're supposed to stop whatever you're doing. If only my parents

33

had listened to that warning . . .' He coughed, turned the engine back on, and that was all he said on the subject.

Time was racing by and Dad suddenly got worried about Newcastle library closing. It was as though something had triggered in his brain and he just had to get there and start looking up his family tree. Actually, I think he needed to be on his own for a while and just didn't know how to tell us. So he was very receptive when I said, 'Just drop us at the B and B, Dad. We really ought to do some more revision, if you don't mind going to the library by yourself? I'll come with you tomorrow to look at it all in more detail.'

'Maybe I should stay with you,' he replied rather half-heartedly.

'Don't be daft, we'll be fine. Anyway, don't you want to see if Mum's rung you back or texted? I don't think there's a signal here . . .' We all got out our mobile phones and checked. No one had any signal at all. It was all that was needed to persuade Dad to drive to civilisation.

'I'll only be an hour or two,' he said. 'And you'll be here revising, won't you?'

'Let's check in and, if you're happy, that seems like a good plan,' I answered, without actually telling him what I intended to do the minute he was gone. I directed him to the bed and breakfast, which was down a tiny country lane right on the edge of Kielder forest. We'd prepaid online, and a very helpful man had emailed instructions for us to just let ourselves in if he wasn't there. Things here were so different to London, where you'd never leave your door unlocked. But as promised, the back door was open and, on the old wooden kitchen table, there were directions to the rooms and instructions to help ourselves to tea and juice from the fridge.

'Time's getting on,' I said. 'You should be going, Dad. We might go for a little walk later, just to the information centre at Kielder reservoir – it's very close. So, if you're at all worried about leaving our things here with no locks, then just bring the bags in when you get back.' He hesitated. 'But no need to hurry,' I added, leading him back to the car. 'We'll just see you here in time for supper later on. I'm excited to hear if Mum's left a message.' That did the trick.

'Okay,' Dad replied. 'But don't wander too far. Maybe get some maps from the visitors' centre and we can work out a nice walk for tomorrow morning. Amazing piece of engineering, that reservoir. You know there's enough water for every person in the world to have a bath at the same time.' Dad got in the car and put on his seat belt.

'What a waste of water,' Mad Dog said. 'Save water – bath with a friend.' He winked at me, but I just turned away, not able to even think of flirting in front of Dad.

We waved goodbye as Dad drove off shouting, 'Enjoy yourselves – stay out of trouble!'

Little did any of us know just how much trouble we were going to find ourselves in before the night was over.

Kielder forest is a massive man-made woodland that surrounds Europe's largest reservoir. The trees cover hundreds of square kilometres and they're all conifers, so it looked more like Scandinavia than any part of England I recognised. The minute Dad was out of sight, I headed straight towards the trees that I knew were between us and the visitors' centre next to the reservoir. I'd looked at maps of this area so many times, I was confident I could find the way from memory. We hadn't even walked two hundred metres before Mad Dog grabbed my arm and made me stop.

'This is a really bad idea, Hattie,' he said. The creepy fog was getting thicker and I guessed it was that and the grey skies that had dampened his spirits – but Neena was looking none too happy either. 'We've turned up here on a whim without a plan and against the express wishes of your mum and Yazuki,' Mad Dog continued. 'I think we should go back and wait for your dad.'

'Neena and I want to explore,' I said, looking at Neena.

'I'm not against it, Hattie,' she said, smiling in a way that I knew meant she was going to agree with Mad Dog, 'but we have to stop and think this through and make sure we all know what our plan is and how to meet up if we get separated. Oh no – did you leave your ninja clothes in your dad's car? What if he finds them? What if you need them?'

I undid my jacket and showed her that I had all my ninja things on underneath.

'Okay, so you're thinking straighter than me on this,' she said. 'At least let's switch clothes while we find out where we are.' Neena was right. We were in enemy territory – we'd be mad not to at least try and confuse them.

Neena and I went behind a tree and swapped our

36

clothes. Mad Dog would normally have teased us about undressing in public, but he wasn't in a teasing mood. He was watching out for anyone approaching – both at ground level and in the canopy of the densely planted trees. 'What's your plan, Hattie? What are we looking for?'

I'd been thinking for weeks about what I'd do if I ever got to Kielder but, now I was here, none of my plans seemed to make any sense. I had thought I'd just be able to open up my mind and the universe would point me towards Mum and Toby. But as I stood amongst these trees, looking for inspiration, none came. I wasn't going to let Mad Dog know I didn't have a clue what we should do or where we should go, so I just called back, 'Let's go to the visitors' centre, get a map and work out a logical way of checking out the whole area over the next two days.' I felt quite safe about going to the visitors' centre, as Kielder forest had lots of tourist attractions around the reservoir. There was water-skiing, boat trips, lakeside walks, all of which happened during the day. It was late afternoon, so all we had to do was to find our way through the forest to the car park and the information kiosk before everything shut at six.

I helped Neena into my ninja jacket, thinking that it was a good job all the clothes were loose. She put on my black trousers but drew the line at my split-toed socks and *tabi* shoes, which I had in one of the pockets. Slightly reluctantly, I let her wear my favourite blue leather pumps, joking that she'd better not spoil them. I easily fitted into her pink leggings and purple mini-skirt and even her shoes with ten-centimetre heels. Her tight, sparkly T-shirt just hung loose on me but from a distance, I knew that I looked like her, especially once I put on her *Save the Whales* baseball cap that she'd got from a charity walk a couple of years before. Lastly, Neena put on my dark blue jacket and pulled up the hood to hide her face.

'Where's the postcard?' Mad Dog called. I took it from the pocket of my jacket that Neena was now wearing and gave it to him. 'Cool threads,' he said, grinning at my new Neena-like image, although we both knew it looked a lot better on Neena than me.

Mad Dog studied the postcard before handing it to Neena. 'Not a lot to go on,' he said. '*Act quick – time running out. TDDT, wage war*, with *Tanil* signed at the bottom. Where do we start?'

'Maybe it's a ninja deceit,' Neena said. 'To get us here, in the middle of the forest with no plan . . .'

'No, I'm sure it's from Toby,' I answered.

'But why would Toby ask you for help?' Mad Dog argued. 'It's crazy, Hattie – he could have come straight to your place from the Foundry when we defeated the Kataki and rescued your mum. But he didn't, he fled. He's one of them. He's a Kataki through and through. If the postcard's from him, then he's probably tricking you somehow.'

An owl hooted, even though it was still only late afternoon. Neena jumped out of her skin. 'The Kataki . . .' she whispered.

'Don't be daft,' I whispered back, for a moment thinking exactly the same thing. 'And don't forget that whatever you think about Toby, Mad Dog, it could have been me taken at birth and kept captive by the Kataki with no idea how to escape them and also —'

'Yes, I know,' he said. 'He killed Mr Bell to save us at the Foundry.'

'Exactly. Why would he do that if he wasn't on our side?'

'Why don't you do one of your mind-merge things and find out what's going on in his head?' said Mad Dog.

'You think I haven't tried?! It's the first thing I do every morning – and the last thing I do at night. I can't get into his head at all – I've no idea what he's up to.'

'Perhaps he's protecting you,' Neena said. 'So you don't know too much and get into trouble.'

Whatever the reason Toby was so elusive to me, I wasn't going to let it stay that way forever.

It started to drizzle as I took the lead deeper into the forest. I knew Yazuki's Chinese medicine friend lived here somewhere. We walked in silence for a while, stopping every so often to listen. I was struggling in Neena's shoes. Mad Dog was carefully noting our surroundings so we could find our way back out. Neena was collecting bits of plants and anything she thought might be useful either to eat or as a healing aid if we got injured. She'd been doing an awful lot of reading about ninja potions and poisons and seemed happy to have the chance to finally pick some of the leaves she'd read about. I could see the pockets of my ninja clothes were already bulging – even the ones where Bushi and Akira were curled up, asleep. It flashed through my mind that I should at least be carrying all my tools and weapons, but none of Neena's clothes had any pockets and I foolishly hadn't brought a bag.

The evergreen trees were getting much thicker. In this misty climate I couldn't even use my eyes to look for signs of anyone following us or some other unusual activity. I'd have to rely on my ears. The wind was picking up – and a strange noise came drifting through the foliage. We all stopped and listened. It was like nothing I'd ever heard before – it was almost like a sound I could *feel* rather than hear. A deep, resonating *clangggg*, like a low, loud gong. The hairs on the back of my neck stood on end. We all looked around, wondering where on earth it was coming from.

Through the mist I could just see a clearing, so I grabbed hold of Neena and signalled for Mad Dog to follow me. At least if we were out in the open, it would be easier to see if someone was moving towards us. Then we heard it again. *CLANGGGG* . . . This time it was unmistakable.

'The bell . . .' Neena whispered, panic-stricken. 'The sign of impending agony, maybe even death. We have to get out of here!' She started to run, but I grabbed hold of her and made her walk slowly into the clearing. The clanging sound got louder. It was very surreal and extremely spooky. It was quite like a bell, but much more haunting and muffled, kind of watery. I signalled for the others to stand still and I closed my eyes to listen. That was when I heard it – a different sound that made my blood run cold. It was far off, but it was unmistakable: flapping wings, huge and frightening.

It was a sound I'd heard before, and I knew exactly where.

My head was filled with the familiar mind-merge image of dark wings and a shadow descending over me. Then sounds started coursing round my brain – screaming, coughing, flapping – and suddenly I knew we were in big trouble. I opened my eyes and just had time to whisper – '*Run!*'

A massive black shape was forming in the mist above our heads, getting bigger and bigger as the spine-chilling, flapping noise filled the air. I kept hold of Neena's arm as we ran, but Neena stumbled. She was never any good at moving fast – I knew that from athletics classes at school. I'd run a few paces before I realised Neena had stopped. She was trying to put a shoe back on, standing in the clearing. I turned back towards her. 'Come on – RUN!' but it was already too late.

The black, flapping shape was swooping right down on top of her. It looked like a bird, but how could it be? It had a three-metre wing span and a long, shining beak. Its claws were the size of daggers and now they were embedded in the fabric of my jacket – which Neena was wearing! My heart was pounding. *What should I do?!* This creature looked half bird, half human – but not like any person I'd ever seen, apart from in my mind's eye. The bird-man seized Neena and plucked her right off the ground, flapping its wings with this noise that made me want to cry out in terror. Without hesitating, I ran after them but they were already three metres in the air.

'Help! Help, please help me!' screamed Nina.

Poor Neena – I knew that whoever he was, this bird-man was really after me.

The haunting, watery tolling bell sound clanged louder, sending more chills down my spine. The wind rushed through the trees. I glanced back at Mad Dog, terrified the bell signalled agony, maybe death, for Neena and it was the last trigger I needed. The bird-man was disappearing high into the trees, his shape getting milkier until both of them were lost in the mist. I didn't pause. I kicked off Neena's high heels and her jacket as I ran, moving easily in her ludicrously short skirt.

'Hattie, don't do it,' Mad Dog called in a strangulated whisper. 'It could be a trap – don't go after them!' But his words fell on deaf ears. Nothing was going to stop me going after my friend Neena, who I felt sure wouldn't stand a chance in a ninja battle, let alone against some evil, vile-beaked bird-man. I shot up a tree and started swinging like a monkey through the forest. I could just hear the flapping of those wings and I wasn't about to give up on my one link to Neena. I abandoned Mad Dog in a heartbeat, just calling, 'See you back at the B and B', like this was the most normal of goodbyes with me running for a bus or late for school.

This bird-man could fly fast, I had to give him that – but I'm not exactly a slouch when it comes to travelling through trees and dropping down to run across the forest floor. Between listening for the tiniest sound of his wings and the occasional cracking branch, I managed to trail them for about ten minutes deep into the dense forest. Neena's tights were ripped and my feet were cut and bleeding and I'd already lost her hat somewhere back near the clearing. My hands were sore as I had none of my ninja clothes or tools

42

and weapons to help me. Words were going round and round in my mind: *You idiot! How could you make so many mistakes, Hattie Jackson!* There was the answer – in my mind I was still Hattie Jackson, fifteen-year-old girl studying for exams and not *Hattori Hachi*, supreme ninja warrior. I was going to have to get my act together pretty fast.

The tolling bell was getting louder, but I was aware of another noise as well. A metallic *swoosh* that sounded every so often. I couldn't place it but if I'd been thinking straight I'd have realised it was a major clue as to what was happening.

Eventually, the trees ran out and I came to an open space. The air was still thick with mist and I could hear no sound of Neena, just some gentle flapping high above me. I felt sure the bird-man must have landed in a tree. I hoped that Neena's silence didn't mean she was unconscious or badly injured. I couldn't let my mind wander to the possibility that she might even be dead.

I crossed to a grassy bank, which rose up above me, extremely high and steep. I silently crawled up it, not knowing what I might find at the top. In seconds, I was caked in dirt. At the top I was surprised to find a road, running left to right. There were no cars or people, so I stayed low and crossed the road to see what was on the other side. As I peered through the mist which was now starting to clear, I gasped.

Water stretched out before me in every direction. It was as though the ocean was waiting for me, here at the top of the steep bank I'd just crawled up. But I knew straight away from the smell that this was fresh water, not salt. This was Kielder reservoir and I was on the dam wall, with the road running across the top of it. The reservoir was as smooth as glass, seemingly stretching to infinity. Set back in the water, about ten metres away, was a high concrete tower. It was modern and really incongruous to its beautiful setting – looking more like an airport control tower than anything you'd expect to see in a nature reserve. I'd read there was a valve tower set into the reservoir – this must be it. It regulated the water level, in case the reservoir got too full.

Something moved on top of the tower – and to my huge relief, I saw it was the flapping bird-man. He was still holding Neena but she didn't seem to be moving and I felt a sudden surge of nausea and fury welling up inside me.

I had to get up to the top of the tower, but I didn't know who or what was inside, so I'd have to be really careful. I'd just decided to ditch my muddy clothes and swim to the base of the tower when I heard something completely unexpected. A low, spine-chilling growl.

'*Toby?*' I whispered, frozen to the spot. And there he was, looming over me. He had on his full ninja outfit, including his hood, but I knew it was him from the noise he'd made – the same growl he always had when he was in his panther animus state. I glanced back up at the tower. The figures had disappeared.

'Have they gone inside?' I called to Toby. 'Can we get to them another way?'

'Follow me,' was all he said as he took off in the opposite direction.

In the very brief time I'd known Toby was my twin, I absolutely believed we were two halves of the same coin. I knew who he was, how he felt, what he wanted – at least I thought I did. So, in spite of other people's wariness of him, it didn't even cross my mind to question him. He bounded off with his panther-strong legs and I was relieved to run after him, even though my feet were still hurting. I felt sure that Toby would find a way to help me rescue Neena. He took the route I'd just come, but now in reverse. As we cut back into the forest I called out, 'I have to find Neena, are you sure this is right?'

He grunted as though to reassure me, and we carried on. I had a million questions I wanted to ask – *What was in that tower? Who was that bird-man and what was he up to?* But there was no time for talking. Eventually, we came upon a tiny dwelling. I couldn't really call it a house as it was more like a mound, set into the forest floor, with grass and leaves all over it, camouflaged like an animal's burrow. But it did have proper doors and windows, even though they were set almost flat to the ground. Toby disappeared round the back and I followed him.

At the rear of the house I stopped and looked about. Toby had disappeared. On the ground in front of me there was an open trap door. I peered down into the gaping darkness, assuming that's where he'd gone. I didn't even pause to question any possible danger as I lowered myself into the hole. I searched for a ladder or some steps with my bare feet, but there weren't any. The ground was wet and suddenly, I slipped. I held on with one hand as I swung my

45

legs, trying to get a grip and propel myself back up, but a shadow fell over me and the trap door banged shut. Excruciating pain shot through my hand and up my arm as I fell, contorted and awkward, down into the hole.

CHAPTER FOUR

'You are only helpless
if you see yourself as helpless.'

I've no idea how long I was unconscious but when I came round, it was pitch black. I'd never experienced such darkness in my life. My head was burning with pain and, for a moment, I panicked, thinking I must have blinded myself. My left hand was throbbing so I felt around with my right, very cautiously at first, gently checking out where I'd hurt myself. It seemed there was dried blood matted into my hair and on my forehead as well – I must have been out cold for quite a while. I could touch walls on all sides without moving from where I was lying. I had one leg folded up underneath me at a very worrying angle and I moved as best I could, easing my bent leg out and wiggling my toes to make sure nothing was broken. My knee was sore and my neck ached, but as I pulled myself up to a sitting position, I was relieved to feel that nothing was broken or twisted. I took a couple of deep breaths, hoping my eyes would soon adjust to the dark. But they didn't. I couldn't make out even a chink of light coming in through the cracks of the trap door above me.

As I felt around, I could tell the space had been lined with bricks and the floor was incredibly lumpy. I picked up what I thought was a rock. It was lighter than I expected and when I sniffed it, I realised it wasn't a rock at all but a lump of coal. Great – so I was probably in a coal-hole and no doubt filthy black as well now.

Carefully, I got to my feet, checking myself again for nasty gashes. By and large, I seemed to be okay. I stood to my full height and felt around. There wasn't a ladder or any way of climbing up. I leant against one wall and used my legs to push against the bricks on the other side, wiggling my way upwards and taking tiny shuffling steps with my feet till I reached the top. I felt around for the trap door and pushed. It wouldn't shift even a millimetre. It was either unbelievably heavy, or it was bolted on the other side. Panic welled up inside me. Here I was, alone in the dark, and no one in the world knew where I was – except for Toby, who for some reason had locked me in this vile black hole and, although he may not have meant to, had knocked me out, possibly blinded me and could even have killed me for all he knew. I so badly wanted to trust him and think he'd done this for my own good, but deep down it was a frightening reminder that he *had* chosen to stay with the Kataki, rather than fleeing them and coming to live with us when he had the chance. Whose side was Toby really on? Was this place part of a Kataki camp? Was there any point in shouting?

It was only then I remembered Neena, limp and lifeless on the top of the water tower with that evil bird-man and his razor sharp beak. My heart began to pound – I had to get out. A scream found its way in my throat and I had to fight to hold it in. Panic and screaming went against everything I'd ever been taught by Yazuki. I had to stay calm and think my way out of this nightmare situation. For a start, there was no point wasting energy holding myself up here by the trap door, so I gently lowered myself down, discovering just how stiff I was and how painful my left hand felt – and my feet, from running all the way through the forest and jumping through prickly trees with no shoes.

It was strange but even as I lowered myself to the ground and tried to find a comfortable position, my brain started worrying about my exams and how I hadn't paid proper attention to Neena's chemistry lesson in the car on the way up. I had to get out of school mode and back into my ninja mindset. I'd already made a big mistake chasing after Neena without making a proper plan with Mad Dog. He must be beside himself out there. I began to panic all over again – what if the Kataki had caught him too? I breathed deeply and shut my eyes. It was so dark that it made no difference if my eyes were open or closed.

Once I was calmer, I gave myself a strict talking to. I had to stop blaming myself for not being on top ninjutsu form and just get back into my Hattori Hachi mindset and remember every one of Yazuki's lessons and all of my ninja training. It was like a lightbulb went on in my head and suddenly I knew I could take care of myself. Hattie Jackson left and Hattori Hachi took over.

Okay, so what was I going to do? What would Yazuki do? What would Mum do? What would Toby do? Mad Dog? Neena? Dad? Dad would use his police radio to call for back-up. I didn't have my mobile phone – I'd left it in the car, knowing there was no signal anyway. And then I thought that any normal person would just shout for help if they were locked in a coal-hole. Maybe that was the best chance after all. Worth a try . . .

'Is anyone there?' I quietly called out. Then a bit louder: 'I'm stuck in here, if anyone can help!'

I hadn't even finished the sentence when I heard a bolt slide above me and the trap door flew open. Light streamed in, blinding me. So at least I hadn't lost my eyesight. The light was so bright I thought it must be the sun, but when my eyes adjusted I could just make out that it was dark outside and the light was coming from a flaming torch. Another mistake. I should have kept my eyes closed and opened them very slowly to acclimatise. I couldn't see who was holding the torch but a ladder slid into the hole. I had no choice but to climb up it. As I neared the top, a hand reached in to help me. It was tiny and gnarled and then a face appeared. It was a very old, little Japanese man. I had no way of knowing if he was a friend or an enemy, but since he was offering me a way out, I let him haul me out of the hole and on to solid ground. He was incredibly strong for someone so small and elderly.

'Hattie Jackson,' he said in quite a strong Japanese accent as I rolled over to look at him. 'Or Hattori Hachi. I've been waiting to meet you.' He bowed. 'You are most honourable, and I offer you my humble service.'

I sat up and bowed back at him. This wasn't what I'd been expecting.

'My name is Takowa Takumi. Yazuki may have spoken of me to you?'

'Hello, thank you, um, no she hasn't.' Well, at least if he knew Yazuki there was an outside chance he was a friend. 'How do you know Yazuki?'

Without speaking, Takumi led me inside his house – if that's what you could call it. On the outside, it was the kind of place a woodland animal might live in – a large mound covered in grass and shrubs. But, as soon as we stepped inside, I gasped in astonishment. It was enormous, stretching far into the hillside and deep underground, with stone cladding on the walls, so it was cool but not cold, and flagstones on the floor and rush mats everywhere so it was clean and homely. Everywhere was lit by flaming torches and candles, creating a very cosy, friendly atmosphere. There were Japanese screens and a low table for eating, with bright cushions around it for sitting on the floor. There was a wood-burning stove to one side, with a chimney and several pots bubbling away on it and Takumi was already ladling what looked like soup into two hand-painted bowls. He put the food on the table and gestured for me to sit. 'Come, eat,' he said.

I didn't need telling twice – I was starving. I did, however, wait for him to eat from his bowl first, pretending I was being polite. He wasn't fooled.

'Yazuki has taught you well,' he said. 'Always wait for your host to show the food is not poisoned . . .' He chuckled and ate from his bowl, then swapped it with mine so I would know for sure the food he was giving me was safe.

I smiled for the first time in ages and then devoured the most delicious soup I'd ever tasted. It was similar to a seaweed soup Neena often made – but this one had even more flavour. *Neena.* My heart froze again and I put down my spoon.

'I have to find my friend, Neena,' I said, rather pathetically, suddenly not hungry any more. 'Someone took her in the forest. I was chasing after her —'

Takumi looked at me and spoke in a soft voice. 'A man running through the forest is chased by a tiger. He reaches a cliff with no other way to escape. There is a vine hanging over the edge. The man climbs down the vine and sees that, at the bottom, another hungry tiger is waiting, his sharp teeth bared. At that moment, two mice appear, one white, one black. Together, they start gnawing through the vine, just out of reach above the man's head. The man sees a wild strawberry growing next to him on the cliff. Keeping hold of the vine with one hand, he reaches across and plucks the strawberry with the other. How sweet it tasted!'

I looked at Takumi, wondering what was coming next. But that was it. He resumed eating and I could see that this was his one bit of advice for me at this distressing time. Okay, so I was definitely back in *koan*-quoting ninja land. *Koans* were the Japanese lateral-thinking puzzles that Mum and Yazuki were both so fond of. I knew Takumi was telling me to live in the present, enjoy the food in front of me and not worry about external threats or what was coming next – but what good was a bowl of seaweed soup when Neena might be being tortured for information she couldn't possibly know because the bird-man thought she was me?! I picked up my spoon and finished my meal as quickly as possible without being rude, so we could move on to finding out about each other.

After we'd eaten, Takumi set about treating all my cuts and bruises. He boiled some water on the open fire for me to wash with and brought me clean clothes. I don't know how, but he found some canvas split-toe *tabi* shoes that fitted me exactly and some rather old ninja clothes that were certainly much better than Neena's ruined outfit. After I'd washed and changed, we sat under a window that was in the ceiling, since we were underground. In fact, it wasn't so much a window – there was no glass in it – but more of an air vent, about a metre square, with four short wooden poles holding up a larger square of turf, so that rain didn't come in but air could. Through the gap I could see the moonlit sky. There were still some clouds which were moving fast, as though the weather was going to stay blustery. I was pleased. Wind and rain are often a ninja's greatest friend – causing noises and distractions that make it easier to confuse the enemy. Rustling trees and lashing rain would help me move around under cover, if I could just find where Neena had been taken.

'Yes, Hachi, bad weather can be a ninja's best friend,'

Takumi said, as though he could read my mind. 'These skies will serve you well before the day is out.' From the few stars I could see, I guessed it was about two in the morning. I wondered whether Dad would have called the police by now. Takumi continued, 'When day breaks, you must focus on the task in hand.'

'Finding Neena, yes,' I answered, relieved we were allowed to talk about her at last.

'No. Finding Neena is not your task and not why you were called to Kielder.'

'Was it you who sent the postcard?'

'No.'

'Do you know about it?' I reached for my pocket, but realised Neena had all my clothes and the postcard as well.

'Yes, I know about it,' Takumi said.

'How?'

'Word has come to me from another route. Has Yazuki taught you yet of *jonin*, *chunin* and *genin*?'

'*Chunin?*' That was the word Mum had said which I hadn't got round to looking up. 'Takumi, can I ask you something before we start on this? How exactly do you know Yazuki? And do you know where she is? She's with Mum and —'

'She calls me her Chinese medicine friend.'

'That's you?' I said, confused. 'You're not in the least bit Chinese . . .' Takumi was nothing like I'd imagined Yazuki's Chinese medicine friend to be – for a start, I'd always assumed her friend was a woman.

He smiled. 'Chinese medicine,' he said, 'not Chinese

friend. Although I am Japanese, I have spent my whole life studying Chinese herbal remedies and poisons, most recently the properties of some rare plants here in Kielder forest. But more than that, I am also a ninjutsu *chunin*. Your *chunin*, in fact, Hachi. I am the one who will pass instructions and train you for the task you have been called here for.'

'Mum has a *chunin* . . . Is that you? They were supposed to be coming to visit you . . .'

'That was just a cover. I am not your mother's *chunin*, no. Nor Yazuki's. There are many middle men − or women − who receive orders from the master at the head of any ninja mission, the *jonin*. Each *jonin* will have numerous *chunin* working for him or her − none of whom are allowed to know who the others are or what they've been instructed to do by the *jonin*. This way, a mission can be carried out from several routes and, if captured, no one can be tortured for information or give away an overall plan as only the *jonin* has that knowledge. I am your *chunin* and I was sent word that someone would lead you to me —'

'Toby?'

'Maybe, but not necessarily,' he said.

'You know Toby?' I asked, eager for any kind of news about what my twin had been up to since I saw him in Camden.

'I know who he is, but I have never met him,' Takumi answered. 'I trust you got a good look at the person who led you here? That you are convinced it was him?'

I paused, feeling my face flush as I thought how I'd recklessly followed Toby through the forest and into the coal-hole without ever getting a proper look at him.

'It was him, I'm sure,' I mumbled. 'But why would he bring me here?'

'To protect you?'

'He could have killed me!'

'It was me who left the coal-hole open, and you who chose to climb down into it. Whoever brought you here may have had no intention for you to harm yourself in this way.'

'They shut me in and hurt my hand.'

'Because they wanted to protect you from your hot-headed self, perhaps?' Takumi answered. 'It must have been clear how traumatised you were about Neena from the way you behaved chasing after her. Whoever brought you here no doubt thought you needed time to calm down and had to prevent you from doing any more foolish things.'

I felt really stupid now, but concentrated on letting go of shame and regret. Neither of those negative emotions were going to help me. I watched as Takumi gently bathed my cuts with thick herbal remedies, massaging my feet and hands. It should have hurt, but the potions were so gentle and soothing – as were Takumi's tiny, gnarled hands – that I was almost glad I'd hurt myself in order to get this kind of attention.

'Should I call you something special?' I asked. 'If you're my *chunin*?'

'Call me by whatever name will make me hear you, loud and clear, and I will come to you if I can. But it's unlikely. You will be going where a *chunin* will find it hard to follow. We're not skilled as field operatives like you are – a *genin*. Your mother and Yazuki are skilled *genin*, too.'

'Yazuki's still a *genin*?' That surprised me.

'Both your mother and Yazuki are far too valuable in the field and in battle for them to be given what amounts to a managerial role.'

'Battle? Are they in danger?'

'Whatever they are doing, people will have been planning for some time and they will no doubt already be deeply immersed in whatever mission they have been called here for.'

'They're both so super-skilled, I'd have thought they'd be at the top of any hierarchy years ago.'

'Don't assume any level of this hierarchy is better than the others. Each person is just suited to their particular title. In the true ninjutsu way, we work as one, each contributing to the greater whole. In normal times, your status as Golden Child designate would mean you wouldn't take part in any risky missions at all. But these are desperate times and, for reasons I cannot know because I don't have the information, our *jonin* has chosen to bring you here to Kielder.'

'Is it to do with Dad? It's such a coincidence – him being born here and now the Kataki being here and Toby and everything . . .'

Takumi shook his head. 'I don't know and I do not need to know.'

'So can you find a way of getting a message to Mum?'

'I didn't even know she'd come here to Kielder, so she must be doing something very secret indeed. I have no idea how to contact her or Yazuki. As far as I can tell, Hattori Hachi, you are very much on your own.'

Great. In that case, I was even more determined to get back out there looking for Neena, Toby and Mad Dog. If Toby had been leading me to safety, why hadn't he helped me out of the coal-hole instead of locking me in there? Where had Mad Dog gone to after I deserted him? Had he been able to get to Dad and if so, had he told him that Neena and I had both disappeared? I was worried that Dad would be frantic, but it was as though Takumi read my mind again.

'No need to worry about your father,' he said. 'He has been sent a message that the three of you are with your mother and will return tomorrow.'

'How do you know that?'

'I am informed of what I need to know. No more, no less. So, Hattori Hachi, after the impetuous mistakes you've already made, can you put your ninjutsu head back on your battered shoulders? Can you make these damaged fingers dextrous again? Will your feet heal enough to carry you wherever your instructions take you?'

'Yes, of course.' I was feeling pretty defensive. 'I've been through quite a lot of training. I should tell you that I fought Praying Mantis and won.'

'This will not impress Raven.'

'Raven?' It was as though a bolt of lightning struck me.

'Others have different names for him: Murderer, Torturer, Slayer, Slaughterer, Demon, Devil. He is a monstrous figure who has terrorised the area for many years, tormenting everyone in his search for the legendary Diamond Dagger.'

'Does he have wings? Huge black ones?'

'He does indeed. He swoops from the skies, stealing sheep to feed his army of hungry Kataki warriors, though some say he doesn't care if his food is animal or human.'

I didn't speak. All I could think was that Raven had Neena and I hoped he didn't have plans to feed her to anyone when he found out she wasn't me.

Takumi sensed my anxiety and continued, 'He took your friend, thinking she was you and by now he will know that you tricked him. He will be furious and humiliated in front of his army. He will use your friend as bait to draw you into his encampment. He is clever and evil.'

'But how did he know I was here – in the forest?'

'He has spies everywhere. I'm sure you will have been followed from your home. There's little you can do without Raven knowing.'

'What does he want from me?'

'Everything that should rightly be yours – or Toby's – on your sixteenth birthday.'

'Why isn't he here, looking for me then?'

'Because whoever brought you to me – Toby or not – was a friend, Hachi. Raven was distracted with Neena, thinking he had captured you. While you are with me, you are safe.'

It was only then that I even stopped to wonder why I'd been so trusting of Takumi. How did I really know he was on our side? But my heart and my stomach told me there was nothing to fear from him. And besides, what choice did I have?

'So is Raven very important in the Kataki?' I asked. 'More important than Praying Mantis?'

'There is no comparison. Raven is more powerful and far more evil. He will attack at random and has no morals. He brainwashes young Kataki so successfully that they will even die for him. And because your victory over Praying Mantis is now legendary, you cannot afford to be complacent. Raven will want vengeance for the way you humiliated the Kataki then, and for how you have tricked him now.'

With that cheery thought, I decided it was time to start getting some specifics from Takumi about what my mission here was actually about.

'Raven has made a camp inside an abandoned castle,' he told me. 'It has a tower that he uses to keep watch over the surrounding area and a high perimeter wall, guarded by Kataki sentries. It's almost impossible to get inside – and that is your task, Hattori Hachi. To infiltrate Raven's camp, find out what he's planning to do and stop him.'

'Thanks,' I said, with more than a little irony in my voice.

'You are most welcome,' he said with no sense of irony at all. Takumi got to his feet and started clearing away the washing things and all his potions and poultices.

'And what do you suppose Raven is planning?' I asked, also getting to my feet – quite astonished how much less painful everything was and how much better I already felt.

'That is for you to find out, as I said,' he answered. 'Your birthday is close at hand. We know he wants the Diamond Dagger before you turn sixteen. The Kataki have been flocking to join him, his army is strong.'

'What do I need to know about this Diamond Dagger?'

'It is legendary. It has the blood of a thousand deaths on its blade. For every person it kills, it takes on more power. It will be the decider of the future.'

'And he wants it now because . . .'

'This dagger is the only way to kill a Golden Child. The person who slaughters you with it will inherit your status and your wealth. It is the only legitimate way to do so – at least as far as the ancient *Legend of the Three Diamond Daggers* is concerned.'

I felt my shoulders go tense. 'Three Diamond Daggers? Slaughter?' Once again, I felt the burden of the Hattori family history bearing down on me.

'Pay no attention to the other two daggers for now. They have been lost for a very long time and are most certainly not in this country. But the one that is nearby will be enough for Raven. It's possible they have risked bringing you here because you will be able to locate the dagger, when so many others have failed. It must be found, Hattori Hachi. But for now, I reiterate to you that your instruction is simply this: Find out exactly what Raven is planning to do and stop him.'

'Couldn't Toby help me with this? He's got as much right to the Golden Child status as me. I just think it would all be a bit easier if there were two of us carrying out this mission together.'

Takumi paused and looked deep into my eyes. 'If Toby does not come over to our side – and we have to accept that he may never do so – and if he inherits the Golden Child status, thousands of innocent people will die. The

61

Kataki stronghold will be so great that they will quickly infiltrate the whole world. They already have training cells on every continent. This isn't just about Kielder or London or your family's land in Japan. This is about possible world domination. It could mark the end of the planet as we know it.'

I just stared at him, wide-eyed. 'And that's supposed to make me feel better, is it?'

'No,' Takumi answered, again completely missing the sarcastic tone of my voice. 'It's supposed to make you understand the exact situation.' He put some powder into a cup and poured hot water on to it.

'Shouldn't I be looking for the scroll before anything else?' I asked. 'I can't become the Golden Child without it, can I?'

Takumi swung round, his face anxious for just a second. 'The scroll?' he said. 'You have the scroll – everyone knows how you tricked Suzi into stealing a fake one.'

'Actually, it was Yazuki who tricked her, not me . . .'

'Nevertheless, you have the original?' Takumi was not his calm self, though he was trying really hard not to let me see how worried he was.

I carried on, perversely satisfied that it was my turn to scare the living daylights out of him. 'It was stolen. Right before Mum and Yazuki came up here.'

'This cannot be!' he exclaimed, really rattled for the first time.

'Yes it can – and it is,' I replied.

'Then I will attend to it,' he said, suddenly composed

again. 'I will contact those who must be told and await instructions. But for now, drink this. It will clear your mind and heal your body of fearful memories that you may have absorbed during last night's terrifying experiences.' He gave me a dark green potion that looked disgusting. I knew I had to take all the help I could get, so I drank it down in one. Surprisingly, it was quite sweet and not at all vile to swallow. A warm glow engulfed me and for a second, all my worries just evaporated. I felt far less exhausted and in brighter spirits all round. Some of my anxiety about Neena and Mad Dog calmed down as well. Everything suddenly seemed clear to me.

Takumi closed his eyes and thought for a moment, then announced, 'You are the focus of all the Kataki's hatred.' Great. Another one-liner to make my heart start pounding again. But Takumi knew what I was thinking and smiled at me. 'If I didn't know how skilled and self-assured you are, then I wouldn't tell you all this,' he said. 'You have nothing to fear except fear itself. Unlike Toby, who has a lot to fear, knowing you should become the rightful heir.'

'Why me?'

'Because even if Toby believes every word the Kataki have fed him since birth, deep down, just from meeting you and your family, he knows you are the most suitable inheritor of the missing Diamond Dagger and Golden Child title – that you are of pure mind and spirit and as yet uncorrupted in the cruellest ways of ninjutsu.'

'But why would Toby want to be the Hattori Golden

Child anyway if that means he'll just get stabbed to death so Raven can inherit everything?'

'We believe that Toby may have entered into a pact with Raven. That Raven does not want him dead because he is a strong fighter with a sharp mind. It has even been suggested that Raven has become a kind of father figure to him and that Toby is already his second-in-command. Raven doesn't necessarily want the Golden Child status for himself, because with that title come so many threats from the families of the other two Diamond Daggers. No, he will want Toby to be the inheritor and then for Toby to stay loyal to him. But they both know you are the biggest threat of all to their plan.'

Of course I immediately wanted to argue once again about Toby not being one of the Kataki. But actually, I didn't have a single bit of proof and was beginning to wonder myself if I could really trust my instincts.

'Shame we can't put Toby and Dad in a room together,' I said. 'I'm sure it wouldn't take two minutes for Toby to want to dump Raven as a father figure once he realised he's got such a fantastic dad of his own.'

'No!' Takumi answered. 'You must never even think of trying to reconcile your father and Toby. The reason is this, Hattori Hachi. We do not know how long this war with the Kataki will go on. You may yet need your father to help you win a battle and that could involve him fighting Toby. He'll find it much more difficult to injure or kill him if he knows he's his son. He will want to protect him in order to get to know him, to make amends for the lost years. And anyway, we don't know yet if Toby will ever leave the Kataki —'

'He will . . .'

'Still, we cannot confuse your father. If the need arises, he must fight Toby and put his life on the line for you, who he believes to be his only child. That's how it must stay until this terrible ordeal is over.' He paused, just to make sure I'd got the point.

'Okay, I understand,' I said.

'All right, Hattori Hachi,' Takumi said, flicking the air around his head with his fingers as though he was banishing bad thoughts. 'We will continue as directed and while you train, I will check with my *jonin* whether this missing scroll situation affects your mission. But first you will sleep and restore your energy.'

It was as though the word *sleep* acted as a knock-out pill. I was overcome with tiredness and I laid my head down on a cushion on the floor. I just had time to feel another pang of anxiety about Neena, along with an overwhelming need to see Mad Dog and to reassure Mum and Dad that I was okay, when sleep consumed me.

When I awoke, it was already dawn and Takumi was standing over me.

'Come,' he said.

Outside, as morning light filled the sky, I had a thrilling few hours' of training. Takumi brought me a pair of stunning hang-gliding wings, made from silk in a deep blue colour which absorbed light in the same way my own ninja jacket did – which of course I no longer had, since

Neena was wearing it. The wings fitted on my body with a rope harness, with toggles attached to strings that allowed me to control direction as I pulled either right or left. Takumi showed me in very careful detail exactly how to tie the wings on and how to operate them, then helped me carry them as we climbed to the top of a tree, over-looking a clearing. 'So now you jump,' he said.

'Then what?'

'You fly!'

I edged further along the branch – and launched myself off without even pausing. I wasn't scared – the wings took my weight immediately. They were light and amazingly aerodynamic. If I used my body correctly, I found I could swoop and turn and glide, then catch a thermal and head right back up again. It was something I'd wanted to do all my life, and here I was – flying!

I couldn't work out how Raven plucked Neena from the ground and took her off into the air like he did; his wings must have had some kind of reinforcement or even some extra power like a motor or an engine. But even as I thought it, I knew it couldn't be true – there was no sound as he moved, other than that quiet metallic whooshing that I'd paid so little attention to.

As I flew, I thought about what Takumi had told me about *chunin*, *jonin* and *genin*. I knew from history lessons at school that this was the principle for many secret spying organisations, like the French Resistance who fought the Nazis in occupied France during the Second World War. They had cells of operatives that knew nothing about what other operatives were doing. Even people within your cell might not have the same information as someone else. They were only told things on a 'need to know' basis so no one could be tortured for the overall plan. I didn't like it one bit. However good my fighting techniques might be, at this moment I wanted to be the one at the top, giving the orders, with all the information available to me about where Mum was and if Neena was okay. At least when I'd been rescuing Mum from the Foundry and fighting Suzi, it had been me working everything out and giving the orders. I also knew that the French Resistance separated out family members, so they wouldn't be tempted to break the rules to try and save someone they loved. I couldn't bear the idea of that happening to us.

This now reminded me that everyone I cared about was scattered around Kielder. I just hoped Dad wasn't in too much of a flap. It was Saturday already. My birthday was on Tuesday. I didn't have an exam till Friday, but even so, if I wasn't back when Dad expected me, I knew he'd have half the country's police force out looking for me.

I flew for hours, managing to keep airborne longer and longer as the training went on. I loved it up here – the thrill of flying and in such a peaceful location. I didn't want to stop, even when it was time to eat, but my mission was fast approaching and I couldn't start out on an empty stomach. Takumi made me a bowl of noodles and as dusk began to settle, I sat with him on the step of his extraordinary home and he showed me my briefing details.

'No word back from our *jonin*,' he said in a grave voice.

'Which means, Hachi, that your mission continues as directed.'

I nodded. 'Of course.'

He unrolled some hand-drawn maps and sketches, all on old parchment-type paper. The first map showed me how the abandoned castle was nestled in the valley below Kielder reservoir. Takumi had drawings of the exterior from all angles, but had never been inside. The map was constructed from information that existed when the castle was the home of a lord over two hundred years before. The castle still belonged to his family so, strictly speaking, no one could enter without their permission. They moved away many years ago and, although the authorities had tried to contact them and the National Trust wanted to take over running it, the family had never responded to any of their requests and the castle remained locked to the outside world.

'That's one family the Kataki have probably won over, then,' I said.

'One of very many locally, I'm sure,' Takumi answered. 'It's hard to know how far and wide their evil has spread. We think they have infiltrators on the council and in the police force around Kielder – schools, universities, probably even in the Armed Forces, who knows? So don't think for a minute that you can go running to the authorities for help.'

The next map had more detail about what Takumi believed was inside the castle walls. There was a lot of land – about a kilometre wide and three kilometres at its longest. There was a river running through the grounds and quite a large lake, though goodness knows what state that would be in now if it had been abandoned for decades. The main castle building had dungeons and a tall tower and there were various outhouses, stables and other small buildings, presumably for staff. Takumi thought that, although the castle must be very run-down inside, its stone walls were strong and high enough to keep out any intruders. To get enough height to fly in over the castle walls, I was going to have to climb the valve tower in Kielder reservoir and launch myself from there. That was exactly where I last saw Neena – with Raven. Even though I was on a mission of my own, this instruction gave me hope that perhaps I could find Neena en route and rescue her, or at least find out where Raven might have taken her once they'd disappeared from the top of the tower. But yet again, Takumi seemed to know exactly what I was thinking.

'Forget everything about Neena,' he said, shaking his head sternly. 'As far as your instructions go, she might as well be dead. Do not try to find her. Let nothing distract you from carrying out your instructions. Although you are our most precious Golden Child designate, you are being entrusted with a highly dangerous and important mission. You are deemed the most capable and talented ninja warrior available to us.'

'Really?' I said, relieved to hear Takumi didn't have a low opinion of me after my impetuous behaviour the day before.

Takumi smiled. 'Yes, indeed – your reputation precedes you.'

'But what do you think Raven will do to Neena?' I was still worried sick, regardless of my instructions.

'It will not benefit you to dwell on things you cannot know,' Takumi replied. 'Someone else will be looking out for her, I'm sure.' But he didn't sound convinced.

'But if I found her by chance, I could rescue her?' I asked.

'I doubt anyone in the world could stop you,' he replied with a smile.

We checked my wings and went back over the plan for me to get into the castle, going over and over what I should look for when I was there. Takumi gave me food and water in containers to keep me going through the night and all the ninja tools and weapons he had, which weren't many. He showed me a handful of plants that could be used as herbal medicine if I found myself badly cut or bruised. He gave me a pen, old parchment paper to write on, some twine and a *hambo* that I tucked into my belt. He wouldn't let me take the maps.

'Memorise every detail,' he said. 'You cannot take them as you must never risk the enemy finding out how informed you are.' Then Takumi led me carefully through the dense trees, back to the reservoir. It took four times as long as when I chased Toby in the opposite direction, but this time we weren't taking any chances.

As we approached the dam wall, the haunting, watery tolling sound was there again – as though warning of yet another tragic death. Or maybe it was trying to warn the enemy I was coming. I tried to shut the noise out, but it was

70

insistent, reverberating through my body. So I just let it wash over me as I made my way towards the water's edge. There was no sign of anyone up on the water tower. It was drizzling now and the wind was picking up.

'Nature is on our side tonight,' Takumi said, with a reassuring squeeze of my hand. 'Now go, child, and may all good things go with you.'

I put on my ninja hood, held my wings high above my head and swam the few short metres to the valve tower. It was hard work and my arms hurt, but I knew soaking wet wings would be useless to me. Takumi had told me there was a ladder up the side of the tower, so I felt my way around the base until I found it on the far side. Holding my hang-glider wings under one arm, I used the other hand to pull myself up the ladder, rung by rung. I started to feel strong and unafraid as I clambered up and on to the flat roof at the top.

I had a quick look round to check for blood or signs of a fight. There was nothing – just a large metal ring set into the side of the tower and some old black fabric heaped up, all wet and dirty. There was no door – nowhere for Raven to have taken Neena. I was quite perplexed. Maybe he'd just stopped here to get his breath back, then flown off in another direction. I put on my wings and went over the plan again in my mind. *Focus your mind, wait for a strong gust of wind,* Takumi had said. *Then launch yourself off down the valley . . .*

The haunting tolling sound got louder, more insistent, as if trying to warn me of something now. I thought of Dad's tears as he remembered his parents' death and the warning he'd given us about the legend of the tolling bell. But then I thought how stupid it was to fear something you couldn't see or touch. People make up stories about anything and I wasn't usually superstitious. I had plenty to fear from actual enemies without adding a haunting noise to my list. This was no time to be faint-hearted. I adjusted my wings, took a deep breath, closed my eyes for just a moment to feel the wind direction – and then I launched myself from the top of the tower. Off down the valley I soared, wind whooshing past my ears, flying high, then swooping down.

Tonight, the blustery wind and rain couldn't have been better for helping me get into the enemy camp without being seen. Although I didn't want the wings to get soaked through, this kind of weather would mean guards would have their heads down to protect their eyes. And the noise of the wind would cause all kinds of strange sounds, distracting them and making my actions much harder to hear. Takumi had said that when I saw the castle, I had to swoop low, using the outcropping trees to obscure me. It would be dangerous flying near foliage because I could catch my wings if I got too close, but that was nowhere near as dangerous as being spotted by a Kataki sentry and shot down with one of the arrows that Takumi warned me they'd all be carrying.

CHAPTER FIVE

'A ninja's mind can soar with the wind.'

It was going to be hard to fight the enemy with these huge wings attached to my back. The only solution was to fly over the castle perimeter wall and then drop quickly into the shadows and hide my wings somewhere.

As the castle loomed larger in my vision, I pulled on the toggle in my right hand. My wings tilted and I swooped to the right. Then I tested the left. My positioning had to be precise if I was going to keep a constant distance from the top of the wall. Even with the rain on the fabric of my wings and the wind gusting me from time to time, I still had terrific control over my movements. I did one big swoop down for good measure, then let the wind gust me back up again. This was some mission!

Flying through the air above a vast forest, swooping down through the darkness towards the enemy camp, I remembered what it was I loved about ninjutsu. I was powerful, I was free – I was possibly the soon-to-be Hattori Golden Child! For a moment, I was confident that everything would be all right and that I'd find a way to defeat the Kataki, rescue Neena and stop whatever Raven was planning. I felt grateful to my parents, proud of my ancestors – of everyone who'd ever been part of my history, allowing me, Hattie Jackson, to become Hattori Hachi, now hang-gliding silently into the heart of Raven's lair. But I reminded myself that pride comes before a fall – and I was a long way off the ground.

A shape was starting to become visible through the misty night air. A hooded ninja figure, walking along the rampart on the top of the stone perimeter wall. There was no way of telling if it was a man or a woman, and in the past I'd learned not to assume anything about the enemy. This one was agile and wiry and held a large bow and arrow, already set for action. Suddenly I wasn't feeling so confident any more. I had to get close to carry out my plan – but I was an easy target up here with no weapons to fight back with.

There was no way I could hang-glide into the castle without being seen. I was still following the line of the trees, knowing that a moving shape would be much harder to see with dense foliage behind than if I was out in the open. I judged the distance carefully and when I saw the Kataki guard turn and start walking away, I seized my moment. Pulling hard down on my right toggle, I veered towards the castle. My heart was racing as I scanned every centimetre of the wall and the land inside. There was only this one guard between me and a safe landing within the perimeter. There were other guards for sure, but they were in the distance with their backs to me. I made my body as streamlined as I could for maximum speed and I soared down towards the Kataki sentry.

Bang! I hit the guard as hard as I could with both feet, then caught a gust of wind and flew upwards again. There was a yell and now I could tell he was a man. He stumbled, then swung round, holding a crossbow up to his eye as I pulled my left toggle and swooped round in a circle, making myself into a ball with my legs pulled up tight to my body as I approached him a second time.

Schooommm! An arrow flew past me, so close to my face it almost grazed me. *Bang, bang!* I kicked as hard as I could and this time I sent him tumbling off the ramparts, dropping ten metres on to the ground inside the encampment. I really hoped he wasn't seriously injured, but that he'd be concussed so that he couldn't call for help, at least until I was inside and concealed.

But *schooommm*! Another arrow shot up from where he'd landed and tore through one of my outspread wings. Suddenly I was plummeting down! Fast and vertical, the ground was coming up to meet me and the air was being forced from my lungs by the pressure of the wind! I pulled on the left toggle, then the right, but neither gave me any control!

My eyes scanned the area below, storing every detail in my mind. It's incredible how perceptive you become with that much adrenalin coursing through your veins. The castle grounds were huge, as I'd expected – and the lake was there, exactly as Takumi had shown me on the map. There was a whole wooded area on the far side. If I kept streamlined and no one else saw me, a tree landing was going to be my safest bet. The wind was picking up even more – which was a real blessing as I caught a gust which momentarily lifted me back up into the air. With just one good wing I only had my body weight to help with direction. I curled into a ball and leant as far as I could to one side. I waited for the wind to sweep me towards the biggest clump of trees, then I stretched out, making myself into a really dynamic arrow shape, pointing straight at the canopy of branches. I was vaguely aware of a rustling sound below – probably the Kataki guard coming to finish me off as soon as I hit the ground. But that was a problem for later. The branches came up to greet me through the mist and damp and I prepared myself for the inevitable agony that was about to come my way.

But I never reached the trees. Something caught my leg and yanked me towards the ground. The guard must have been nearer than I'd thought. I tried to relax, knowing this was the best way to fall, but it wasn't easy to let go of all my muscles when the ground was hurtling towards me at such a ferocious rate.

My body was totally unprepared for what happened next. I hit the ground, but my body kept on falling! It was as though the earth was swallowing me up. Eventually, I slowed down, and then I started heading right back up to where I'd come from – it was just like I was on an oversized trampoline! At least my bones weren't broken, but I had no idea how my leg had been caught or who was waiting for me in the shadows. As I dropped back down again, only to bounce back up, I pulled the *hambo* out of my belt, ready to fight.

'Whoa, there . . .' I heard a voice whisper. 'Just keep bouncing, Hachi, you're okay . . .' The voice was familiar, and only a few people in the world knew me as Hachi. A figure appeared but I kept my stick held up in front of me, ready to attack if I had to. 'Hachi, Hattie – it's me!'

It was Mad Dog! I'd never been so relieved to hear someone's voice in my life! He caught hold of me and stopped me from bouncing, then quickly untied my wings and pulled me into the trees. He hid my damaged wings at the bottom of a pile of similar ones that were stored on a wooden pallet, along with the rope he'd used to lasso me. Then he took my hand and led me into the thickest area of foliage.

'How did you get in?' was all I could think to say.

'Later,' he whispered back. 'We have to hide.'

As we made our way round the edge of the landing area, I could see exactly what had happened. By chance, I'd flown right over a massive trampoline that was set into the ground – presumably so Raven had a soft landing every time he came back. Mad Dog had lassoed my leg and pulled me on to the trampoline.

He pulled back some bracken, covering a dug-out pit in the middle of the trees. We jumped in and dragged the bracken back over so no one would suspect we were there.

'Knew right away it was you,' Mad Dog whispered, pulling off my ninja hood. 'I'd recognise that double leg kick of yours anywhere!'

'What happened to that guard?' I whispered. 'Is he dead?'

'No, he was the one who shot the arrow at you after he'd fallen. I didn't know whether to attack him or help you. But then someone else appeared and gagged him and dragged him off. You've got friends everywhere!'

'Was it Mum?' I said, my heart racing.

'Didn't see,' he answered. But it lifted my spirits to know that maybe Mum or Yazuki was already in the camp. Or maybe we had other allies.

There was a snap above, as though someone had trodden on a twig, and we both froze. We listened for what seemed an age but there wasn't another sound. It might have been the wind or it could have been one of the Kataki guards patrolling the grounds. We took it in turns to put our mouths to each other's ears so we could whisper, hardly making a sound. I loved feeling the warmth of Mad Dog's neck as I told him all about Takumi and my mission and the *chunin*, *jonin* and *genin*. I explained why I wasn't looking for Neena now. I felt so bad, just leaving her with goodness knows what to deal with. But Mad Dog had some news on the Neena front.

'Raven taking Neena off through the trees was a trick,' he whispered. 'It was fabric on a pulley that went through the forest to the top of the tower – and you followed.'

'Fabric? What do you mean?'

'That's what you chased. Just some black material that looked like Raven and Neena, flying through the trees on a zip wire – a decoy while Raven actually took Neena off in the opposite direction.'

'So that's what the whooshing noise was? The metallic sound? Just a zip wire?'

He nodded. 'If you'd waited two seconds, you'd have seen you were being fooled. I called and came looking for you, but you went off like a bat out of hell . . .' Then for good measure and to prove he was still my old friend, Mad Dog nudged me and whispered, '*Loser.*'

But I was in no mood for jokes. I gripped his arm, desperate for some good news. 'Where did Raven take her? Do you know?'

'They dropped into a hidden passage. I went after them, but I haven't seen either of them since I've been in here.' There was another sound, a muffled cough this time, and we both froze again. We sat in the darkness, waiting. There was so much I wanted to ask – I still didn't know how Mad Dog had got inside the castle grounds. But we both knew we were pushing our luck, hanging out in the heart of the Kataki training camp with sentries all around. By the sound of it, some of them were arriving to check over the hang-gliding wings. I just sat there gripping Mad Dog's arm, thinking back to all those hours we kept watch from our pit at the Foundry and how the two of us had faced terrifying ordeals before and survived.

Eventually, things went very quiet outside. Mad Dog gave me a squeeze and kissed the top of my head like he so often did, then he gingerly peered out from under the bracken. The wind had dropped and the sky had cleared quite a bit. There was enough moonlight for us to see the trees looking pretty still. Mad Dog slid the bracken cover to the side and climbed out. He beckoned for me to follow, keeping his back to me and continually looking all around so that he didn't risk missing something – or someone – nearby.

We made our way silently through the trees, sometimes crawling across the woodland floor, sometimes climbing up and moving through the branches. All those hours of training with Yazuki had paid off – both of us could practically fly from branch to branch without making a sound. As we worked our way around the camp, I managed to get more sense of the layout. It was just as Takumi's map had suggested: a large, imposing castle with a tall tower to one side with extensive grounds, a lake and a lot of woodland. I'd felt sure the lake would be overgrown, but it was completely clear of any weeds or plants. The edges were trimmed and it was just this large expanse of water. At the far end was a wooden tower about five metres high with what looked like a large lamp on top. All very strange.

What Takumi's map hadn't shown was what was obviously a newly constructed building at the edge of the clearing in front of the castle. It was a beautifully-symmetrical, one-storey Japanese building with a simple pagoda roof. It looked as if there were two long rooms, one each end, jutting forwards at a slight angle from the large, central area. In front of the furthest room there was a hole dug

80

into the ground, giving off a red glow. There was a massive spit above it with a whole carcass roasting on it. I paused, just staring at it, remembering what Takumi had told me about Raven not caring if his prey was animal or human. Then I shuddered and whispered, '*It's a sheep*'. I couldn't bear to even contemplate the alternative.

We crept around to the back of the building to look inside. The nearest long room was obviously the sleeping block. About forty Kataki were lying on their rolled-out mattresses. Everything was sparse and clean. Two guards were keeping watch at the far end. We moved silently to the back of the central area. As we peered inside, we could see the big, main space was a dojo for ninjutsu training, with tools and weapons on the walls and mats and small trampolines lining the floor. Mad Dog's eyes lit up. I knew what he was thinking – that we could arm ourselves from here. But I shook my head. Those weapons would be under heavy guard. Even if there wasn't a person watching over them, there were sure to be invisible wires to alert them to intruders, or 'nightingale' floorboards that were designed to make a chirruping sound whenever anyone trod on them. I nodded for Mad Dog to follow me as I carried on to the far room, which I felt sure was the kitchen, given the barbecue pit in front of it.

My guess was right. A shaft of moonlight illuminated a long wooden table with a stack of flat wood blocks on it – the type sometimes used as plates. There were beakers for drinking and a jar with lots and lots of chopsticks as well as a wall of kitchen knives, ladles and other utensils. A few massive pots were stacked, clean and shiny, on a surface next to where the embers of a wood fire were gradually dying out. The embers gave off enough light to let me see there were two bodies on the floor, both with their backs to us, sleeping. At first I couldn't make out whether they were guards or prisoners, but then I saw that one of them had huge, rusty leg irons clamped round their ankles, with a chain about half a metre long joining the ankle bands and another longer chain, which was padlocked to a massive metal ring on the wall. I recognised those blue leather shoes immediately and grabbed Mad Dog so hard he nearly yelped.

'*My shoes!*' I mouthed at him. '*It's Neena!*' Mad Dog prised my fingers from his shoulder as I pointed, excited.

'*Could be a trick,*' he mouthed back at me. But I knew Neena's body shape and now I was convinced those were her ankles with cuts and bruises from the bands of metal. But at least she was here – and alive! I couldn't see who was next to her, but knew it might be a Kataki guard.

Mad Dog and I settled in a tree, high above the wooden dojo, to think. We had to have a plan. With most of the camp asleep and the guards keeping watch over the sleeping area both upwind of us, it felt safe to speak again.

'My mission,' I whispered, 'is to find out exactly what Raven's planning to do and stop him. I've been forbidden to get waylaid rescuing Neena.'

Mad Dog nodded, looking deep into my eyes, knowing straight away that not helping Neena would be the hardest thing ever for me.

'Of course I want to get her out of here,' I said, 'but I can't risk us getting caught.'

'Maybe I can help out then. Since I haven't been given a mission. Perhaps I can rescue her and get her out of the castle grounds.'

'How?'

'The way she came in? The place where Raven attacked us was right by a hidden entrance into an overspill tunnel that runs underground from Kielder reservoir,' Mad Dog whispered. 'I think it's there in case the reservoir gets too full, so they can get rid of the water, maybe out to sea. It doesn't look like it's ever been used, but it runs under here. That's how Raven vanished so quickly. I only found the way in by searching and searching after I stopped to ask myself what it was I'd actually seen. It's how I got in.'

'Through an overspill tunnel?'

'Yes. It's gigantic – twice my height and the same across. You could drive a double-decker bus through it. I followed it all the way to the reservoir at the top, then I came back down, searching every centimetre till I found another door that had been cut into the tunnel wall. *That's got to be the Kataki*, I said to myself, *putting doorways where they weren't intended.* It was locked, so I waited until it opened and two ninjas came out with some bin bags. They headed away from the reservoir and before the door swung closed, I ducked in and found myself in the castle dungeons. I knew you'd turn up eventually.' He grinned. 'We'll get this cracked, Hachi, don't worry. And we'll get Neena out. Promise.'

There was a clanking of chains in the kitchen. Then the sound of a pan being filled with water.

'I bet Neena's talked her way into cooking for the Kataki,' I whispered. 'To stop them killing her or locking her up in the dungeons.'

We climbed down and crept to the open window. Neena turned to put a pan down on the long, wooden table and I waved frantically to attract her attention. The look on her face said it all. She just grinned and tears welled up in her eyes. I pointed to the person sleeping on the floor and made a thumbs-down sign to see if they were the enemy. She shook her head, silently pushing the window wide open, beckoning for us to come inside. We climbed in. I hadn't taken two steps before I knew exactly who was lying on the ground. I'd have known that quiet, irregular snore anywhere.

'Dad?' I whispered, looking at Neena. She nodded and shook him awake. His bleary eyes opened.

'Mr Jackson,' she whispered. 'Hattie's here. Don't make a sound!'

He rolled over – and didn't look at all surprised to see me. He nodded his head as if to say hello, but he couldn't actually speak because his mouth was gagged.

Things were getting stranger by the second. Dad, Neena and Mad Dog were all inside the castle, when I'd had to nearly kill myself to get in!

'What does he know?' I asked Neena, making a sshhh sign to Dad as I untied his gag and cut the ropes binding his hands and feet.

'Nothing,' she answered. 'He was tied up and gagged when Toby brought him in. They gave him something to make him sleep and he hasn't woken up since.'

That explained why Dad wasn't responding properly and looked so dazed. I didn't have a clue what to say or what to do. This wasn't how ninja missions were supposed to be – Dad was the last person I was expecting to see and right now this felt more like a family camping trip gone horribly wrong. But there was worse to come as the next family member appeared. It was Toby, arriving without a sound from behind a silk screen that was placed across the door from the barbecue area. He took one look at me and stopped in his tracks.

'Wondered how long it would take . . .' he said.

I took a breath, knowing that the next few seconds would probably tell me whether Toby was on our side or not. It could mean the difference between life and death for me.

'I know you're not going to let anything happen to us, Toby,' I whispered. 'I need you to help me get Neena, Dad and Mad Dog out of here, then to show me a safe hiding place.'

He stared at me, giving nothing away. My heart was in my mouth. 'What makes you think you stand a chance in here?' he said, smiling, but with dead eyes. I still couldn't read any sign of what he was thinking or feeling.

'You risked your life to kill Phil Bell to save me, remember?' I was pretty glad Dad was groggy and couldn't follow what we were saying. He wouldn't know what to make of this, especially as he still had no idea that Toby was actually the son he thought was dead.

'I wouldn't save you if you were the last person on earth,' Toby said. 'You tricked me at The Foundry. You let me take a fake scroll . . .'

'That was Yazuki. And, anyway, you killed for me. Actions speak louder than words.'

'Really? What does this action say then?' He pushed away the silk screen and an enormous shadow fell over me. Someone was standing there, lit by the moonlight, so I could only see them in silhouette. I knew that hateful shadow though – I'd seen it many times before. It was a rat, with brutal teeth and a long, disgusting tail . . . The very same animus from the fight when Mad Dog had nearly drowned in Camden canal. My stomach churned and my palms began to sweat.

Standing a metre from Mad Dog was Phil Bell.

CHAPTER SIX

'See others through your knowledge of yourself.'

Mad Dog didn't even take a breath. It was pure, terrified instinct that made him kick his leg out and send Phil Bell flying sideways into a stack of shiny pots. The Kataki would be on us in seconds. I wasn't about to give in without a fight, but my brain was seriously confused. I'd based my whole theory about Toby being one of us good guys on the fact that he had killed Mr Bell at the Foundry to save us all. And here was Mr Bell – alive, with his rat animus as putrid and evil as ever. And boy, was he a vicious fighter. He grabbed an industrial-size cooking pot in each hand, flinging them at Mad Dog with ninja precision. But Mad Dog must have had enough adrenalin coursing through his system for everyone in the room. He ducked down so the pots skimmed past his head, then he rolled over towards the wall where all the knives and utensils were hanging.

Every thought in the universe ran through my mind – from what Dad would be thinking, to whether Neena was okay, to how on earth we could fight a Kataki army and still get out alive.

I had truly believed that Toby was one of us, but right now he didn't seem to have our best interests at heart. He saw Mad Dog moving towards the utensils and immediately propelled the silk screen right between them and Mad Dog. I could already hear movement from the dormitory opposite, so I let go of all distracting thoughts and just got stuck in. I used an old trick that Yazuki had taught me, cartwheeling across the room, grabbing a stone doorstop in one hand as I passed over it and a wooden bucket with the other as I righted myself. I hurled them at Mr Bell without pausing. I got two direct hits – one on each leg. He buckled and fell like a dead weight to the floor. I could have aimed for his head, but I really didn't want to kill anyone if I could help it. Next, I ran at Toby and jumped high, aiming for his chest. But he was too fast for me. He side-stepped and I found myself flying through the air towards the red embers of the fire. I bounced off the wall above the fireplace and backflipped with my legs flying over my head to the sound of Dad shouting.

'Hattie, what the —?'

'Owww!' Mad Dog yelled, as a rolling pin hit him square in the stomach, courtesy of Toby again, who'd grabbed the nearest thing that could be used as a weapon. I hadn't realised how much these two were spoiling for a fight – but they were going at it now, hammer and tongs. Mad Dog grabbed the rolling pin and used it like a club to fight Toby, who fought back with a metal ladle that he grabbed from a hook on the wall, eyeing the row of knives that were on the other side of the room. As Mr Bell pulled himself back to his feet, Neena stretched her chains across the kitchen, slamming the main door and wedging a broom handle across it to stop the Kataki getting in. I knew that would only give us a few seconds – but I had an idea. Mr Bell's legs were still hurting and he was weak.

'Dad, FIGHT!' I yelled, not expecting him to act straight away. But he did – he grabbed a poker and swung it at Toby. Toby leapt out of the way and, for a second, he caught my eye. I could have sworn he was begging me not to let Dad hurt him. But it was just an instant, and then he was firing wooden blocks across the room at all of us like some hot-shot at a funfair side show.

I wished I could have shouted to Dad, 'Don't hurt Toby, he's your son!' but Takumi's words resounded in my ears: *'We cannot confuse your father. If the need arises, he must fight Toby and put his life on the line for you, who he believes to be his only child.'*

My eyes scanned the room. I'd never considered what a dangerous place a kitchen could be. Neena was doing great work with the chain that held her fixed to the wall. As Toby ran towards Dad, she pulled it taut and tripped him. Suddenly his panther shadow emerged and his eyes shone red. It could have been the embers from the fire reflecting, but it wasn't the first time I'd seen this happen. Now Dad really had no idea what was going on as I leapt on to the long wooden table, somersaulting the length of it to cross the room as fast as possible to beat Toby to the wall of knives. Mad Dog was firing eggs at Mr Bell and Neena was throwing potatoes as I rolled off the end of the table and high-kicked at Toby who had come round to meet me. He caught my leg, but I twisted my whole body and, spinning around, I brought my other leg up and kicked him in the chest. I sprang into a backflip, pulling both legs away and catching Toby on the chin as my legs flew over my head. I just caught sight of Dad looking astonished as I landed the right way up and grabbed a knife. I went straight for Mr Bell and, catching him round his neck with my left arm, I brought the knife up under his chin with my right.

'No one move!' I yelled, my heart pounding. 'Except you, Dad – there are weapons in the training room next door!' Dad disappeared and I looked around. With me holding a knife to Mr Bell's neck, everyone was still. There were Kataki at all the windows and, for the moment, Neena's broom was still keeping the door barred shut. 'I don't know what he's worth to you,' I said, pulling the knife closer to Mr Bell's throat for maximum effect, 'but he means nothing to me. Actually that's not true – I thought he was dead and that suited me just fine.'

Mr Bell let out this pathetic little whimper as Toby laughed, stepping towards me.

'You're done for, small fry,' he jeered. We looked at each other, eyeball to eyeball. My heart was aching. I was desperate for some small sign from him that he was faking all this aggression. But as he spoke, his eyes gave nothing away. 'Are you going to kill him?' he sneered. 'I don't think so . . .'

To be honest, I didn't know what I was going to do, but Mad Dog was there to help me out.

'If she doesn't, I will,' he said, brandishing an even longer knife. He squeezed my arm with his other hand, knowing how distressed I must be feeling about Toby. There was a tiny noise and I turned just in time to see Dad, a crossbow held taut in front of his face, lined up on Toby's chest. I didn't even have time to open my mouth before he pulled the trigger.

Schoom! A silver-tipped arrow shot towards Toby's heart! No, no! If that arrow hit Toby, he'd be dead for sure! I didn't even stop to think. My reflexes kicked in and I threw my knife, timing it exactly to intercept the arrow just ten centimetres from Toby's body. There was a clash of metal on metal as the knife flew up into the air, sparks everywhere, and to my enormous relief, the arrow deflected into the wall. Everyone looked in surprise and shock – Toby most of all – as my knife came spinning down and landed with a *thwang*, embedded in the wooden door frame right beside Toby's head. It was enough of a distraction for Mr Bell to grab Mad Dog's arm and throw him to the floor, dislodging his knife from his hand as someone kicked the door open, breaking the broom handle in two. Kataki poured in through the windows and doors. Toby just stared at Dad, then me, realising he'd been only milliseconds from certain death. Dad had tried to kill him and I'd saved his life. It was quite a lot for him to digest.

'Good shot, Dad,' I said, as each of us was grabbed by a hooded Kataki, dressed in black.

Dad just looked at me, speechless.

Mr Bell was beside himself with glee. 'Oh Toby, Toby . . .' he taunted, giving me a creepy look. 'Seems you've got a secret admirer who can't bear to see you hurt.' He laughed in a really cruel way and stared right at me. 'Letting your emotions get the better of you is rather a pitiful weakness for a supposedly gifted ninja warrior,' he jeered. He turned back to Toby. 'Where should I take them? The dungeon?' He grabbed a handful of my hair and pulled it so hard, my eyes watered.

'No!' Toby snapped back. 'Take them up to the tower. Guard them. We'll deal with them later.' With that, he pulled my knife from the door frame and stormed out past Dad, grabbing the crossbow from him as he passed. He didn't look either of us in the eye.

Mr Bell and the Kataki manhandled us towards the door, leaving Neena still chained to the wall. As I glanced back, I saw two Kataki grabbing her, while Mr Bell took great delight in propelling me violently outside. The carcass on the barbecue loomed large as he pushed my face down towards its head.

'That would be too good a punishment for you,' he said. It looked nothing like a sheep now and I shuddered, wondering what terrible fate might be in store for us all.

Mr Bell took us across the open eating area and into the tall tower. We were all dragged up a stone spiral staircase and at the top there was a room, about four metres square. It had nothing in it but a bucket and some thin mattresses rolled up in the corner. There were windows on three sides and glorious views if you were feeling in the mood for surveying the castle grounds and beyond. All the windows had bars, about the width of a hand span apart. The Kataki threw us into the room without a word and locked the door.

Dad looked at me for a moment. 'Okay, start at the beginning and don't leave anything out,' he said, trying to sound calm. 'But before you start,' he continued, 'just tell me one thing. What's going on with Toby? And what on earth is Phil Bell doing here – I thought he was dead!'

'There's so much to tell you, but there are things I've been told to keep secret,' I said.

'Enough, Hattie!' Dad barked. 'These people are trying to kill us and I want to know why!' He just stood there, staring at me. My mind raced through a million scenarios of how I could get out of telling him the truth, how Takumi had told me not to let him know who Toby was under any circumstance, how even if someone was to tell him, surely that had to be Mum. But standing there at that moment, recalling the look in Dad's eye as he aimed his crossbow at Toby's heart, I knew beyond doubt that not telling Dad was going to cause us a lot more trouble.

'You can't kill Toby,' I said. 'You can't hurt him or hate him. You can't do any of these things, Dad – you have to be prepared to die for him, like you are for me.'

Mad Dog just stared, guessing what was coming. I took a deep breath and finally said what I'd wanted to tell him weeks ago.

'You have to love him like you love me, Dad, because Toby is your son.'

I'm not entirely sure what reaction I expected. In my mind's eye, we always told Dad this epic news once we'd found Toby and brought him back home. I'd imagined it a million times and in every scenario – whether it was me or Mum who told him, or maybe even Toby himself – Dad's eyes welled up and he'd either cry or laugh and certainly hug Toby and say that he'd always dreamed of this moment and even wondered from time to time if this was the case, since Toby looked so like me – half Japanese, half English. What I hadn't imagined for a second was what he actually said.

'That's a lie. My son is dead – I heard his screams as he perished in the fire. He died and we buried him and, whoever that evil boy is, he's tricking you and playing with your mind. Don't ever mention this again, Hattie.' He turned away, like that was the end of the conversation.

I was stunned. Even though Mum had warned me the news could trigger a big emotional response in him, or that he might even deny it, I just didn't expect that he would ban the topic without even asking a few questions.

'So how do we get out of here?' he said abruptly, checking all the bars on the windows.

It was at this point that Mad Dog decided he and Dad could do with a man-to-man chat.

'It's okay, Ralph,' he said, taking Dad's arm and pointing to the floor. 'Why don't we sit down and I'll tell you everything while Hattie comes up with a plan?'

And tell Dad he did. He explained how I was a truly gifted ninja warrior and that I'd been training in secret as my ninjutsu persona, Hattori Hachi. He described in great detail how the Kataki had been living in the tunnels under the Foundry and how Mum had been abducted by her own half-sister, Suzi, who was also Praying Mantis, the most deadly assassin on earth. While Mad Dog talked and Dad listened, sitting on the cold floor with his back to the wall, staring into space, I went over every centimetre of our prison room, looking for ways we might be able to escape. I checked in the bucket and rolled out the mattresses to discover each just had a small, thin blanket inside and nothing else – not even a pillow.

'The thing is, Ralph,' Mad Dog said eventually, 'there's some pretty weird stuff going on and what I've learnt is that you just have to kind of go with it and know that Hattie is about the best equipped fighter in the world to deal with whatever's thrown at her. None of us want her to get hurt, but I promise you, we don't have to try and protect her either. She's incredibly skilled and can pretty well look after herself.'

There was silence for a few moments, then Dad eventually said to me, 'Ever since your mum disappeared last year and especially since she came back, I've guessed there were things the two of you hadn't told me. But these people are weirdos – some kind of deluded sect – and I forbid either of you to engage with anything to do with them. We need to get out of here and inform the authorities.'

'They've infiltrated the police,' Mad Dog said, but I shook

my head to silence him, knowing that going along with whatever Dad said was the best way for him to digest everything.

'I agree, Dad,' I said, 'but every one of these window bars is set deep into the stone walls and they're solid metal and I don't have any of my tools or weapons. The door has an old-style lock that would take a hefty key to open.' I pointed to the ceiling. 'These roofs are tiled with heavy slate, so even if I had a way of getting up to the ceiling and holding on, it's unlikely we could work our way through to the roof above. The blankets are thin and small, so there's no chance of knotting them together even if, by some miracle, we could get out through one of the windows.

'That's the reason Mr Bell didn't bother handcuffing us or chaining us to the wall – there's zero chance of us going anywhere. And anyway, I hope that by the time I've finished telling you everything I know, you may agree that we should stay here for now anyway, so that I can try and fulfil the mission I came here for.'

Dawn was breaking – a beautiful, still morning with birds singing and the distant sound of sheep. We sat talking, filling Dad in on as much as we dared. I felt okay telling him all about Takumi, my *chunin*, and the news that Raven was after a long-lost Diamond Dagger. He seemed to believe all this without too much argument. But whenever I mentioned Toby, Dad flinched, like his blood was boiling, so I was careful not to say anything about the family connection for fear of sending him into a rage again.

In return for all this family ninjutsu information, Dad had some news of his own.

'Well, I had a really productive time at Newcastle library,' he said, all cheery, as though it was something of a relief to be getting back to a normal topic of conversation. 'I found some old records about Kielder reservoir.' His eyes started to shine as he described how the village where he grew up had been deliberately flooded when the reservoir was made. All the inhabitants were evacuated in the late 1970s when Dad was just seven years old.

'As you know, that was a terrible time for me,' Dad told us, but this time he wasn't tearful. He talked in a matter-of-fact way. 'Moving out of the only home I'd ever known, my parents killed in a car crash soon after, being sent to Yorkshire to live with my uncle's family. But do you know what? All the abandoned buildings from my village are still down there. Including the church with the bell tower. Hey, and you'll never guess what I discovered – that noise you sometimes hear, the strange tolling sound that everyone says predicts agony or even death? It's not a warning sign or anything like that!' He laughed. 'There was a cross-reference to an article in *New Scientist* that says it's just when the reservoir level drops and the wind's in the right direction – it creates a current that causes the sunken church bell to swing and make that wobbly, watery tolling noise.'

I glanced at Mad Dog, remembering us freaking out when we heard that noise just before Neena was taken. Dad carried on, excited by his research. 'Apparently, most of my family were campanologists. Bell ringers,' he added. 'Wouldn't mind having a go myself sometime.'

'Where is the village then?' Mad Dog asked. 'Because

we heard that noise and it didn't sound like it was coming from nearby.'

'It's not so far from the valve tower that rises up by the dam wall. It's in the middle of the widest part of the reservoir. There was a diver's report that said there are all kinds of buildings, even a stone bridge still down there, in line with the little jetty they use for water-skiing boats now. I went to have a look when I found you weren't at the B and B.' He paused and I could tell the reality of our situation had hit him again. He searched in his pocket for a torn off page from a notepad. At the top there was a picture of a stone cottage with the name *Cragside B&B*. Someone had written – not Dad because it wasn't his handwriting – *Kids okay, with Mum tonight, don't worry, will call tomorrow.*

'They told me your mum rang and left this message. That's when I started worrying,' he said. 'How would she have known where we were staying unless she'd got the message I left on her mobile and, if that was the case, why on earth wouldn't she have phoned me? Do you think they've got her locked up somewhere?' he said.

'No,' I replied straight away. 'No, Dad, I really don't think Mum's in trouble. I think she and Yazuki are fine because, if they weren't, the whole mission would be stopped and someone would be here to get us out.' I didn't believe a word of what I was saying, but I didn't see any point in worrying Dad any further at the moment.

'Tell us more about your sunken village,' Mad Dog said, enthusiastically. 'Do you remember it from when you were growing up?'

'Every detail.' Dad smiled. 'I was a very happy child – well, until I was seven. I loved the house I was born in. You'll never believe what I was going to do when I left the library, before I got distracted by the note. I was going to swim down and have a nose around.'

Mad Dog couldn't believe his ears. 'How far down is it then?'

'Five, ten metres – it depends on the water level. That's no problem for me. I love the water – I was a police diver for over eight years.'

'Wow,' said Mad Dog. 'I never knew that.'

'Me neither,' I said, thinking that there was still so much I didn't know, on both sides of my family.

'Not something I talk about much,' Dad explained. 'Mostly to do with dredging lakes and rivers for dead bodies.'

'Did you find some?' Mad Dog loved anything gruesome.

'More than it's healthy for any man to see, yes. Mostly in cities, some in the Thames and generally adults, though there were a few children.'

I hated hearing about children when the police were involved, it was always distressing. I changed the subject back to the matter in hand. 'But you didn't swim down to the village, so what did you do? How did you end up in here?'

'Well, I did walk to the lake, thinking that was the direction you said you'd be heading. And that's when all this strangeness started. I caught a glimpse of something in the sky – a shadow, like a hang-glider, but it was dusk and so not really time to be up there. So I followed this giant bat thing, running as fast as I could, but it dropped out of sight and didn't come back up again so I kept making my way to where I'd last seen it and then I hit a high wall. Stone. So I started climbing.'

'Climbing?' said Mad Dog. 'How?'

'Crampons,' Dad said, pulling a mountaineering version of a climbing claw from his pocket.

I could have kissed him right there and then. I grabbed it from him. 'Where did you get this, Dad?' I yelped.

'Climbing shop. In town. Thought I might take you up to White Crags on Kielder Head Moor. It's a great climb – I did it a few times with my granddad when I was a kid.'

'But you don't climb!' I said.

'I did. Till I had you to look after and your mum forbade me to take risks.' That made me laugh, considering all the risks Mum was taking – and encouraging me to take as well. Dad pulled out a second crampon. 'I did sprain my ankle once, mind – trying to do a climb in the Lakes when I hadn't prepared and wasn't really that fit.'

'Dad, I can't believe what a genius you are,' I said, 'smuggling climbing claws in.'

'Nearly didn't survive to smuggle anything in. Those walls have been treated with some kind of anti-climb material. Nothing I could see, feel or smell, but the crampons just wouldn't hold.'

'Takumi said it was impossible to get inside by climbing,' I told him. 'So how did you end up in here?'

'Someone must have been laughing their head off, watching me from up above. Didn't think for a minute there'd be sentries watching out from the ramparts. But this guy . . . wow, don't know how he did it. Must have been on a rope, but he slid down, silent and invisible . . . I'd just slipped back down for the umpteenth time and there he was – *bam!* Chopped me on the back of my neck and, next thing I knew, I woke up with Toby staring down at me in the kitchen. My hands and feet were tied and he was pouring liquid into my mouth. Don't remember much after that.' His whole body tensed up again. I could tell he was furious and confused and really ready to fight Toby, or anyone else who so much as looked at him.

'Good job it was Toby who was with you, not Mr Bell or Raven,' I said. 'He obviously didn't check your pockets, or if he did . . .' I paused. I dropped my voice to a tiny whisper so there was no chance of the guard outside the door hearing. 'Well, then he wanted you to keep these climbing crampons because he knew they might help us.'

Dad snorted like that was the most unlikely thing ever.

'Dad, you have to know that I believe that Toby is my twin and that he doesn't want us to die in here.'

Mad Dog couldn't stop himself. 'If we're all giving our honest opinions, I think he's definitely one of the Kataki,' he whispered. I swung round to stare at him, cross that he'd express any doubt in front of Dad when I already had the hardest job in the world, trying to persuade Dad not to hurt Toby.

'Thanks, Mad Dog, but this is family business,' I said.

'No it's not. My life's at stake as well here, don't forget. You have to let go of any idea that Toby's going to help us. He didn't kill Mr Bell back at the Foundry and it's obvious they're on the same side now.'

A shadow passed across the east-facing window, big and black, momentarily blocking out the light. I felt the sick knot of terror back in my stomach. We all moved over to see what was going on outside. It wasn't Raven but another hang-gliding ninja warrior – one of about twenty, all swooping through the air, filling the sky. It was amazing to watch as they wove in and out of each other's paths until one huge, terrifying bird-man figure suddenly appeared high above them.

'That's Raven,' I whispered. He was dive-bombing, trying to send the others crashing down to the ground.

'It's like he's testing them,' Mad Dog replied.

'Who is this Raven man?' Dad asked, craning his neck to see. Another flash filled my mind and I felt a searing pain as the memory of my mind-merge with Suzi overtook me again. There was screaming and flames and I knew for sure it was Raven I could see in my mind's eye, at the hospital where I was born, flapping his huge wings. But I knew it wasn't the time to discuss the hospital fire with Dad, so I banished all thoughts to the back of my mind.

'He's their leader,' I said. 'But like most leaders of renegade organisations, he's power-mad and deranged. As far as I can tell, he's seriously emotionally damaged and I don't know what's caused him to be like that, which worries me. *Fight your enemy's weakest points*,' I continued. 'That's one of the first rules of ninjutsu. To beat him, I have to know him, and I don't.'

'And he's got some terrible plan because Hattie's supposed

to find out what it is and stop it,' Mad Dog added.

'It's a training camp, isn't it?' Dad said, as the hang-gliders moved around outside the window.

Mad Dog nodded. 'Pretty likely, I think.'

'Although he doesn't seem to be doing any traditional ninjutsu training at the moment,' I said. 'It's like he's training these people specifically for flying.'

We spent the next hour or so watching the Kataki outside our windows, diving, gliding and landing on the trampoline about twenty metres below us. Dad worked out that to get the height they were arriving at, they must all be coming from the reservoir tower. Eventually, I admitted that's how I'd got in as well. He nodded slowly. Still looking out of the window, he said, 'I understand there's a lot I don't know about you, but this is hard for me, Hattie. I'm your dad. I'm genetically programmed to worry about you and take care of you. So however much you tell me not to, that's not going to change.'

'I know. And you do take care of me,' I said, putting my arm through his.

On the ground below, about ten Kataki were now doing shape-shifting exercises and drilling themselves in tools and weapons. Their skills were truly breathtaking.

'Those are his hardcore ninja warriors,' I said. Outlines of snakes, reptiles, insects and other creatures fell across the ground as they moved, each in their own particular way. Then Toby appeared and we heard – and felt – his deep rumbling roar.

'How does he do that?' Dad asked.

'Years of practice,' I replied. I had to laugh as I turned and looked at Mad Dog, who was now trying to show off to Dad. He had the climbing crampons and he was suspended above the door where the guard couldn't see, with the claws dug deep into the ceiling's wooden cross-beams. He was holding some string across the top of the side window to make his spider's web shadow and he was doing a fantastic spider impersonation. Dad saw the shadow before he saw Mad Dog. He looked up at him, his mouth half open.

'That's pretty impressive, son,' he said.

'Thanks,' said Mad Dog, jumping back down. 'There's no way we're getting out through the ceiling though. Those slates weigh a ton.'

'You're impressive too, Dad,' I said. 'You were a police diver and you climbed mountains – what else don't I know about you?'

'Quite a lot. And you know what? All sorts of things are starting to make sense to me now. It was your mum who begged me to stop doing dangerous police work. She never explained why, except that we had you. I thought she was just frightened that something might happen to me. But if this is what her family's wrapped up in – this kind of . . . what did you call it?'

'Ninjutsu.'

'If this is what her family spend their time doing, no wonder she wanted me to step down from life-threatening police duties.'

'Absolutely,' I agreed. 'If it was Mum's idea for you to shift to community police work, I'm sure it was because she needed to know you were always going to be there for me if anything happened to her.'

Dad held out his arm and I moved in under it. I may be a special ninja warrior who had a very important mission to accomplish, but I was still a fifteen-year-old girl and never one to turn down a fatherly cuddle. The way Mad Dog was staring, I could see he badly wanted a cuddle too. I wasn't sure if that was because he wanted to be the one comforting me, or whether he wished he had a dad to look after him when he needed it. I held out my other arm and he came over so I could put it round him. He took my hand and squeezed it. We stood there in silence, me, Dad and Mad Dog, watching Raven and his army of flying ninjas and contemplating where we were and what needed to be done.

Eventually Dad sighed. 'Don't see the crime, see the person. That's what they taught us in the force. Seems ninjutsu and police work aren't that different. Try and understand what motivates someone, because that will tell you their weaknesses and instruct you how to defeat them.'

'What do you think drives Raven?' I asked.

Dad slowly shook his head, as outside, Raven dive-bombed another hang-glider. 'He's a classic bully. He's afraid of something – they always are. That's why they have to be so brutal, in charge of everything, obeyed.' Raven's victim lost control and was careering dangerously towards the trees. The person crash-landed in the canopy, jettisoned their wings and scampered off like a monkey.

'Yazuki!' I whispered. Mad Dog Dog leant nearer the

window to see, but the monkey figure had already disappeared into the foliage, dragging their wings out of view.

'Was it her?' Mad Dog, said, hopeful for a moment. But I couldn't be sure.

'I hope so . . . and I hope not,' I said. 'I want her to be here, but I don't want her to be injured . . .' Suddenly the enormity of everything hit me. I wasn't getting anywhere with my mission and I had no idea if Mum and Yazuki were even alive. I hadn't seen Neena since she was being manhandled by two brutal Kataki as we were dragged away from the kitchen, so I had no idea what had happened to her either. My heart sank and my mood dipped.

Suddenly Mad Dog stepped away, energised. 'Okay, Hattie needs to focus,' he said. 'We've all got to be at the top of our game for whatever comes our way.' He pulled me to the middle of the small room, then took Dad by the shoulders and moved him in front of the door. There was a barred window at eye height and Mad Dog positioned Dad so he blocked the view of anyone looking in.

'There's likely to be some fights, Ralph,' Mad Dog said, running up the wall and doing a backflip for good measure, landing without making a sound. 'We've both been training really hard.' He made as if to fight me hand-to-hand, somehow wanting to prove to Dad we were both really good. I stepped back. I didn't want to overload Dad with all our ninja skills. But Dad's eyes lit up.

'Show me that move you did again, Hattie – when Toby grabbed your leg?'

It was the excuse I needed. Secretly, I'd been dying to

106

show Dad some of my ninja moves and, to be honest, I was bursting with nervous energy, cooped up in this cramped little space, worrying about Neena, Mum and Yazuki. I didn't want to draw the guard's attention to us, but luckily Mad Dog and I had done all our training with Yazuki, who always insisted we fought in absolute silence. Without making a sound, I lunged at Mad Dog and aimed a kick. He grabbed my leg and I spun my body horizontally, flinging my other leg up and catching him in the chest. I carried on with the twist, wrenching myself free from his grasp and flipping my whole body backwards, doing a cart-wheel in the air without putting my hands on the ground. I landed perfectly on my feet. But I didn't stop there. I ran at the wall, took a step up it and did a backflip, picking up the bucket as my feet flew over my head and propelling it straight at Dad.

'Catch!' I whispered, and he did. He got the idea right away, not making a sound either. '*Now hit me with it!*' I mouthed. To start with, he was very timid, aiming the bucket about ten centimetres from my face. I whispered, 'Come on, really slug me!' He swung the bucket behind his head and brought it towards me. I blocked his arm with mine, punched him in the stomach – not too hard – caught his hand that was holding the bucket, twisted his wrist and took the bucket from him like candy from a baby. He fell to his knees, silently yelping. So, for good measure, I turned the bucket upside down and put it gently over his head.

Mad Dog laughed. 'Haven't lost it then,' he whispered.

'Wish Raven was here, I'd show him what for,' I answered.

Mad Dog lifted up the bucket. 'You okay, Ralph?'

Dad rubbed his arm and got to his feet. He looked proud as punch at me. 'Job for you in the police force,' he said. 'Any other tricks up your sleeve?'

I could see the mountaineering crampons were still in the wooden ceiling beams where Mad Dog had left them. 'Leg up!' I said to Mad Dog and he cupped his hands in front of his body. I ran at him, stepped on to them and jumped up to the ceiling, grabbing the crampons. Mad Dog crossed to block the window in the door as I pulled myself up. I let go of one of the crampons and slipped my foot into the strap instead. Then I let go with my hands completely and put my other foot in the second one. Now I was walking across the ceiling, like this was nothing out of the ordinary at all!

'And for your next trick?' Dad said. 'I hope you've got a plan because I sure as hell don't know what to suggest. I'm obviously the novice here . . .' On cue, as if by magic, something wonderful happened. As I paused by the south-facing window, completely upside down, a familiar face appeared.

It was Bushi! And she was climbing in through the bars! Behind her came Akira. They both had tiny rolled-up pieces of paper in their mouths.

'Oh Bushi!' I exclaimed, never more pleased to see her in my life. 'Hello Akira – thank goodness!' I released my feet one at a time, putting my hands in the crampons to turn myself back up the right way, then dropped down to the floor, picking up a cute little rat in each hand and giving them each a kiss and a hug. I gently took the paper from their mouths.

'They were in my ninja jacket pocket,' I said to Dad, as though this would explain everything. 'They must have found a way to hide all this time – they're the smartest rats on the planet! And if this paper is a note from Neena, then things are definitely looking up!'

CHAPTER SEVEN

'Suspicious eyes only see evil . . .'

The rolled-up pieces of paper were carrying two messages from Neena – which was a relief on several counts. First, it meant she hadn't been killed after we were dragged away from her. I'd been struggling not to think those dark thoughts, but the anxiety had been there, bubbling away. Second, it meant that maybe she had a plan of some kind. She had written – in tiny letters – on one piece: *Toby has postcard. Heard them talk about still looking for scroll.*

'Maybe someone just took the scroll for safe-keeping,' I said to Mad Dog and Dad.

'Thirty-six hours to your birthday, though,' Mad Dog said. 'Either you or Toby has to have it in your possession —'

'Or what?' Dad asked.

'Or neither of us becomes the Golden Child and we can't change anything – the fighting and destruction will go on until there's another chance for someone to become the Golden Child,' I answered.

'Yes,' said Mad Dog. 'Yazuki's been doing loads of research. If the scroll isn't around the moment the inheritor turns sixteen, the whole rigmarole happens again in seven generations' time and meanwhile the Kataki carry on with their horrific behaviour.'

'But the scroll's not my concern right now,' I reminded them. 'I just have to find out what Raven is planning to do and stop him. That's all. Everything else will be taken care of.'

'We hope,' added Mad Dog, sounding less than sure. 'I think Toby's taken the scroll and hasn't told anyone because he wants all the wealth and power for himself and doesn't even want to share it with Raven . . .' He trailed off, remembering it wasn't a good idea to talk about Toby. But he needn't have worried – Dad wasn't listening. He was staring at the second piece of paper, squinting.

'Neena's eyesight must be exceptional,' he muttered. 'How can she write this small? Think this is a *P* – oh, *Planning*, yes, that's what she's written. There's something else . . . No, can't read it – what does that say, Hattie?' He handed me the tiny piece of paper and I went to the window to get the best light on it. It did say *Planning* and what followed was perfectly clear the minute I laid my eyes on it.

'*Explosion*,' I read out. 'Looks like they're planning to blow something up.'

Dad and Mad Dog just looked at me.

'Like what?' said Mad Dog.

'And where?' added Dad.

I paused for a moment, wondering what Neena's message might mean.

'Takumi said they want the Diamond Dagger,' I said. 'So presumably, they're going to blow something up to try and find it.'

'Let's get out of here and get the police on the phone,' said Dad. 'Or the army – this mob need locking up, they're a bunch of terrorists.'

'That's not going to work, Dad. If we bring the police or army in, the Kataki will just go underground again and wait till it all dies down, then do whatever it is they're planning anyway. Even if this lot were all locked up, there's another thousand to replace them. By all accounts, these cells of underground ninja warriors are forming all over the world. They've already infiltrated the police, the army, local councils, and probably governments as well. So we don't even know who we can trust.'

'All for a dagger?' Dad said.

'Hard to believe, I know,' I answered. 'But these legends mean everything to them, especially to a man like Raven. He obviously feels very hard-done-by somewhere down the line. Our best way of stopping a catastrophe is to try and find out exactly where the dagger is and retrieve it. And we're best placed to do that from the inside right now, at least to find out exactly what they know and what their precise intentions are.'

'Weird this is all happening where you grew up, isn't it Ralph?' Mad Dog said. 'Makes you wonder if it really is a coincidence.'

'I can assure you my family has nothing whatsoever to do with these villains,' Dad scoffed, totally unaware how wrong he'd turn out to be. But I was sure there was a connection too, particularly since Dad had been born in the village that was submerged in the reservoir.

More than anything, I just wanted to get out of that ridiculously small room and have a snoop around to see if there was any clue at all about what Raven and the Kataki were planning.

We all dozed for a while, leaning against our cell walls, catching up on some much-needed rest. When we woke, Dad was full of suggestions about how to call in our guard, then surprise-attack and overpower him. I knew that we'd more than likely get caught and that would just cause them to double the number of guards and make escaping twice as difficult. But it turned out Neena was already one step ahead again.

It was lunchtime – I was starving as I realised I hadn't eaten for ages. From our east-facing window, we could see the clearing where the Kataki all gathered to eat their meals. We were taking it in turns to check on our guard, watching them every so often through the barred window in our prison door. Mr Bell had been outside all morning, with an ever-changing shift of Kataki who each wore a red belt over their loose black trousers and ninja jacket when they were on guard duty. They seemed to put on the belt when they had possession of the key – which was on a long chain, attached to a metal ring that was sewn into the belt. They wore their black ninja hoods all the time, so the belt not only meant the key wouldn't get lost, but it made it easier for everyone to know who did what and who had keys. Through one of the windows we could see people wearing various belts down below – there were different colours for different sentries, guards and keyholders. Anyway, ours was in red and it was time for his lunch, so a stand-in guard came up the stone steps. The stand-in looked very skinny and uncertain – no doubt one of the untrained youngsters that Raven had brainwashed to come and work for him.

As I peered through the bars in the door, I could see the belt being handed over. Our original guard went downstairs with Mr Bell and I crossed to the window to watch them come out of the tower at ground level and go to join the thirty or so Kataki outside, all sitting cross-legged on rush mats in the eating area below.

Suddenly, there was a noise above us – like a giant animal scuttling on the roof. A dark shadow loomed and Raven swooped down past the window, doing some very impressive aerial acrobatics, just for show, then landing in the middle of the semi-circle on the trampoline. About six of them ran in to catch him and help remove his enormous wings. It was odd that, even with his wings gone, he still wore a bluey-black layered cape that gave the impression of feathery wings, so he still looked bird-like and vicious.

'Did you see how he landed?' I whispered.

'Very shaky on his legs,' Dad said.

'Lopsided,' Mad Dog added. 'Not at all elegant for someone who's so nimble in the air.'

I nodded. 'His left side is weak,' I said. 'Look at him.'

Everything was ant-sized below us, but even so, we could clearly see two Kataki helping Raven as he limped to the rush matting to sit on the ground for his meal. Then I saw Neena, making her way towards him, hobbling herself now, with the chain still joining her feet to each other and the leg irons weighing heavy on her ankles. One by one, she served food first to Raven, then to the guards on his left and right, then round the semi-circle, struggling back and forth to the kitchen, bringing out wooden block after wooden block with food on.

'I'm starving,' groaned Mad Dog. 'Think we'll get anything?' His answer came about twenty minutes later, when we heard chains rattling on the stairs that led up to our room.

'Sounds like Neena,' I said hopefully. And sure enough, as I peered through the bars in the door, there was Neena outside our door with three wooden blocks balanced precariously on her arms, each with some food and a small beaker of water on it. We heard the sound of a key in the lock and I stepped back. The door swung open and the young Kataki stepped in front of Neena, not about to take any chances by letting her come near us. He shouted something in Japanese, holding out his hands to take the food, presumably so he could pass it to us himself. But, as Neena reached the top of the staircase, she misjudged the last step and tripped, sending our food and water flying all over the guard and on to the flagstones outside our cell door. She yelped as the rusty irons dug into her tender ankles – but Mad Dog yelped louder.

'Our lunch!' he shouted, as Neena's body sprawled across the flagstones at the top of the stairs.

She was already shouting, 'Sorry! Sorry!' as the Kataki guard leapt back, unintentionally pulling on the chain attached from his belt to the key in the lock. The key flew out and tumbled to the floor, exactly where Neena was already scooping up wet, sticky rice and trying to pile it back on to the wooden blocks. She was crying and begging, 'Please don't hit me!' to the guard, who raised his metre-long *hambo* over her head, about to hit her, as he brushed the sticky rice off his ninja clothes with his other hand.

Neena gave him the key back and bowed at his feet. 'Forgive my clumsiness, I'm not used to being chained,' she said. Not one word rang true to me – but that was because I knew Neena. The guard was completely taken in, enjoying the fact that she was grovelling. But Neena hadn't finished yet. 'Please can I bring these people fresh food and water?' she asked, imploring him with her big brown eyes.

'They eat what you brought and nothing else!' he ordered. Neena started crying all over again as she finished scooping up the rice. Dad bristled. I knew he wanted to grab this guy and punish him for treating an innocent schoolgirl with such brutality and contempt. But I caught Dad's eye long enough to give him an almost imperceptible shake of my head, letting him know not to do anything. I was sure Neena was in complete control of the situation. She gathered up the cloths that had been covering the rice and laid them back over the meals, her body blocking the guard's view of the trays. Still on her knees, she passed the blocks to us one by one through the doorway, then bowed her head. If her performance so far had been good, then the best was yet to come.

'Please forgive my clumsiness and eat what you can of this lunch,' she said, talking in a dramatic way that sounded nothing like the Neena we knew. But the tears of apology were welling up again. 'I fear, though,' she continued, 'that you should eat nothing because of what your food has now been in contact with. But please, in true Zen style, gaze at your meal in careful contemplation of the care and thought that went in to its preparation and its delivery to you and then eat of it what you will.'

So that was it. The food had something special about it that we were to look for. Neena stepped back and the guard slammed the door. We heard him put the key back in and heavy-handedly lock the door. Then we heard Neena bravely hobbling back downstairs as fast as her leg irons would allow.

Dad was wide-eyed. 'What was all that about?' he asked.

I checked the guard wasn't looking through the bars of the door. I took the cloth covers from the meals, one by one. 'Brilliant,' I whispered. 'Neena, you're a ninja extraordinaire!' There, in the middle of my pile of sticky rice, was an imprint of the key to our door. Clear as day. I could see exactly what it would take to construct a key that we could insert into the lock from our side and that would turn the mechanism that was keeping us all prisoners here.

Mad Dog nodded and smiled and even Dad was

impressed. I didn't waste any time. I took a couple of metal grips from my hair and used a wooden chopstick that Neena had delivered with lunch as the main rod of the key. With Mad Dog's piece of string, I quickly attached the hairgrips at exactly the right distance from each other and made each one the right length so they would turn the elements of the locking mechanism. I could see from the big, clunky key imprint that this was not a sophisticated lock, but an old-fashioned, very straightforward mechanism, as long as you had the right length and number of prongs to turn the barrels. As soon as the key was crafted, I mashed up the sticky rice to destroy the evidence, then hid the makeshift key inside my clothes and shouted, 'This food is inedible! Tell your master to send us a replacement!' Our original guard was just arriving back, taking the belt from the young one. I heard murmurs as the situation was explained, but the older guard just laughed.

'Eat or go hungry,' he said dismissively through the bars on the door.

'*If only they knew*,' I mouthed to Mad Dog and Dad. '*It's us who should be laughing.*'

We had no choice but to wait now till dark. I spent the time thinking carefully about all the options that might present themselves if the key worked and I was able to get out and have a proper look around.

Dad couldn't keep quiet, he had so many questions. He kept coming back to how long Mum and I had known about the Kataki and exactly what had happened all the time Mum had been missing. I didn't want to tell him too many things that might upset him – not yet, anyway. And besides, I thought Mum should be the one to answer a lot of his questions. So Mad Dog deflected most of the difficult subjects by asking Dad about his police training and demanding more and more stories about gruesome police investigations. When Dad's stories dried up, Mad Dog just chipped in with anything that came to mind. He told Dad about his difficult childhood, about his dad beating him and his mum dying when he was young – even how terrified of water he was and how Mr Bell had once tried to drown him. I could see Dad was getting more and more fond of Mad Dog as the hours went by. He sat closer and closer to him, said flattering things and called him 'son' a couple of times. I felt pleased – and very impressed with Mad Dog for being so honest and open about himself and for protecting me from difficult questions from Dad, especially when I needed some thinking time.

I should only have been thinking about my mission and ninjutsu techniques for stealth and fighting, but I have to admit I did find myself also reflecting on how nice it would be if it was just me and Mad Dog here, sitting quietly, preparing to sneak out together. Over the last year, Mad Dog had got to know me better than anyone – even Mum. He'd been with me all through my early training and he understood me. He never gave me a hard time like Dad often did. He always knew exactly what I needed and what I was thinking. And he was a great kisser. I knew that from the night at the Foundry. As he talked to Dad, smiling and laughing, I couldn't take my eyes off his lovely lips.

'Hattie? What do you think?' I heard him saying. 'Ralph says maybe he and I should go and look around?'

'No way,' I said and my reveries were broken. 'No way, Dad! You have to stay here. Mad Dog and I know how to do this and you could jeopardise things . . .'

'Okay, calm down,' Dad answered. 'We'll think it through. But I'm not happy about you going off without me right now.'

Mad Dog signalled for me to let it lie. 'We'll work out something that everyone's happy with,' he said in his self-allocated role as negotiator.

We waited until it was dark and Raven had finished putting all the Kataki through another round of night-time flying. In the moonlight, we could see that Mr Bell was very involved this time. He seemed to be marking out plans on the ground, using a stick to draw shapes. He drilled the Kataki over and over, marking routes for them, pointing to where they'd fly and where they'd land. I guessed this was all to do with the explosion they were planning. From this high up we couldn't begin to get any details of their mission. Eventually, they all headed to the dormitory building and things went quiet. I knew there would be sentries on duty as there had been the night before, but they were some way away and not in our direct line of sight. The only guard we had to worry about was the one outside our door. I hoped that he would eventually start dozing. We unrolled our mattresses and settled down as though to sleep, each with a blanket over us. Dad dozed fitfully, but Mad Dog and I took it in turns to get up and move around the walls, out of sight of the door, peering through the bars to see what the guard was up to on the other side. We could just make him out in the semi-darkness, lit by a flaming torch at the top of the staircase.

On one of his checks, Mad Dog gave me the thumbs up. I swiftly rolled each of our mattresses loosely to make the nearest shapes to bodies that I could and placed them next to Dad, lined up, so his body was between them and the door. I put our blankets over the mattress rolls, hoping, if anyone looked, that in the dark they would pass for two sleeping prisoners. Then I shook Dad awake. I knew from years of experience that when I woke Dad from sleep I had a few minutes to get him to do whatever I wanted. He always took a little while to wake up properly.

'Curl up to these two mats as though it's me and Mad Dog,' I whispered almost silently. 'It's the best thing you can do to help, Dad – don't let them know we're not here.' He looked sleepily at me just for a second, then his eyes opened wide. He remembered where he was and, panicking, he looked across to the door.

'Dad, you have to,' I whispered. 'We don't have time to argue.' I held my breath, just waiting, while he came round to realising he wasn't going to win and that, if he stalled a second longer, we might lose our only chance to get out. Obediently, he curled his body as though he was snuggling up to me, holding my blanket in such a way that it looked like my rolled-up mattress was me, underneath it. He also had hold of Mad Dog's roll and from the door it really looked like the three of us had curled up together for warmth.

I moved back into his eye line and gave him the thumbs up and he mouthed, *'Take care, love.'*

I mouthed back, *'You bet.'* I crossed to the door, silently slipping my makeshift key into the lock. Mad Dog watched, holding his breath. I knew this key had to be exactly right as it wasn't strong enough to force the lock. If the grips weren't in exactly the right place, it wasn't going to work. I glanced through the bars to check the guard was still snoozing, then I gently revolved the chopstick that was attached to my hairgrips, deep inside the lock.

I jiggled the chopstick very slightly, feeling the barrels inside turn one by one. There were four separate elements and I felt them give – one, two, three . . . Something caught and, for a moment, the chopstick was blocked. I jiggled again and magically – *clunk* – the fourth barrel turned. I pulled the door handle and it opened. I'd paid attention at lunch – the door was silent until it was open about thirty centimetres, then it gave a nasty creak. Mad Dog knew this too, so the moment we could both slide sideways through the opening, we did. I pulled the door closed, inserted the key and locked it from the outside. I didn't want to risk the guard finding out we'd managed to unlock the door. We needed to have a good look round, find out as much as we could, then let ourselves back in to our prison before sunrise.

It only took seconds for me and Mad Dog to make our way down the huge spiral staircase. We were really good at this now – silent and invisible, me in Takumi's ninja clothes and Mad Dog in his black clothes and balaclava that he took everywhere with him. We had one of Dad's climbing crampons each, figuring that if either of us was caught, the other would at least still have one. It was hard to believe Toby had searched Dad and not found them. It made me think once again that he had deliberately let Dad keep them because he wanted to help us.

From Neena's note, it was obvious she'd heard the Kataki discussing plans for an explosion. Since I had to try and find out what Raven was planning, Neena was the obvious person to ask. This wasn't going against anything Takumi had told me. When we reached the bottom of the tower and emerged into the cool night air, I signalled for Mad Dog to follow me to the wooden dojo. We moved in silence, straight to the back window where we'd first seen Neena nearly twenty-four hours before. I'd had all afternoon to think how I was going to release her from those horrific leg irons. I knew they were cutting her ankles and giving her a lot of pain. But I had a plan and it was simple and quick – always the best type of ninja action. Instead of going in through the kitchen window, I cut through to the back of the big, central room which had all the tools and weapons stored in it. As I'd looked in yesterday, I'd noticed all kinds of horrible chains and handcuffs. I was hoping one of them may have the same key as Neena's leg irons. Just as I expected, they were all still there. Some had keys in the locks, waiting for their next victim. I studied them for a moment, wondering which of these keys might fit. Then I saw it. Of course! One solitary key, dangling by its string on an otherwise empty hook – the storage place for Neena's leg irons when they weren't in use! No one was expecting us to escape our prison, so they had no need to hide it.

I took Akira from my pocket and traced the shape of the key in the soil. I gave the sign for *fetch* and my clever little rat slid in through the partly open window and ran across to where all the leg irons and chains were stored. In seconds he was running back towards me with the correct key in his mouth. I took it and he slipped silently back into my pocket.

Mad Dog waved for me to hurry. We crept back along to the kitchen window. I was relieved to see Neena was alone in the kitchen, exactly where she'd been before. She was lying as though she was asleep, but I knew she was awake. She was on her side with her back to us and her arm over her head. I knew Neena well enough to know she can only sleep lying flat on her back. I didn't speak or try to communicate, I just made my way over and gently touched her shoulder. She moved her head just enough to look at me. She smiled and gave the thumbs up.

I put the key into the lock of the leg iron on her right ankle and turned it. It fell open. The same happened with the one on her left foot. She pulled her legs up under her, rubbed her ankles and carefully stood up. She let out a huge sigh of relief. Mad Dog silently brought a sack of rice and put it where Neena had been. There was a dirty blanket on the floor, so I laid it over the rice and the leg irons, so the only thing showing was the chain that joined them to the wall. The three of us moved back to the window and silently climbed out. Mad Dog was the last through, grabbing some bread on the way out. I was so hungry I took some from him, knowing a ninja should never fight on an empty stomach. But then Neena went one better. She reached back inside and took a ladle of soup from a huge pan, passing it to Mad Dog who drank it hungrily. Then she did the same for me. It was delicious – seaweed and tofu with a delicate fragrant taste. She dropped the ladle back in, then took some leaves from her pocket – ones she'd collected from the forest – and put those in as well. She shook her head and pointed at the food, letting us know that we shouldn't eat any more of it. I didn't waste my breath asking why.

We made our way back to the bracken-covered pit where Mad Dog and I had hidden the night before. All three of us crowded in and I reached in my pocket and took out Bushi, then Akira, and gave them some bread I'd saved.

It was only then I noticed that Neena had something under her arm. It was my ninja jacket, giving off its magical bluey-black glow, even here in the semi-darkness. Until now, none one of us had spoken. Eventually I decided it was safe.

'So they're planning an explosion?' I whispered to Neena.

'I saw boxes of explosives in the cellar when they brought me in.'

'And what did you hear about the scroll?'

'Just heard Raven screaming at Toby that he had to find it and if he didn't, Raven would inflict a punishment so painful, Toby would wish he'd never been born.'

'Poor Toby . . .' I whispered. I caught Mad Dog and Neena glancing at each other.

'Okay, Hattie, I have something to say and you've got to listen,' Neena said. Even though she was whispering, she still managed to use that tone that I know not to argue with. 'You *have* to tell your dad about Toby – you can't keep messing everything up by jumping in to defend Toby whenever your dad has a go at him!'

'I know,' I answered. 'I've already told him.'

Neena just stared at me, open-mouthed. 'What did he say?'

'He didn't believe me. He's in denial, furious. He thinks Toby's messing with our minds, so there's no guarantee he still won't try and kill him if he gets half a chance.'

Neena grimaced, but Mad Dog was getting impatient.

'We don't have long,' he said. 'Come on, what's our plan?'

'We need to look around,' I whispered. 'Find out exactly what it is they're up to.'

'Let's go down to the cellar,' Neena said. 'Get a better look at those explosives.'

'Are there guards?'

'Don't know. They brought me clockwise, then up some steps over there.' She pointed towards the castle. 'There was a lot I didn't see down there.'

'Okay,' I answered. 'Once we leave here no one speaks. Signs only – and if we get into trouble, split up. Neena, this is the key to your leg irons – whatever happens, get yourself back to the kitchen and lock yourself back into them and pretend nothing's happened.' I gave her the key and turned to Mad Dog. 'If you and I get split up, meet back here and we'll let ourselves back into the tower together. Okay?'

They both nodded.

I pushed up the bracken and checked no one was about. I listened for ages, waiting to hear whether any animals or insects were making a noise or any birds suddenly moved in the trees. Nature has a great way of communicating whether anyone's moving around. But there was nothing out of the ordinary, so eventually I climbed out of the pit. Neena followed. Lastly, Mad Dog sprang out and dragged the bracken back in place.

I put on my ninja jacket, so happy to feel the familiar fabric next to my skin. I gave Neena the one Takumi had given to me, emptying the pockets of all the paper, tools, herbs and poultices Takumi had provided so that I now had everything useful stored about my person. I was relieved no one had searched us when we were taken prisoner and hoped again that it was because Toby wanted to give us the best chance of escaping and taking him with us.

It was odd seeing Neena dressed ready for ninja action, but she'd really earned her place – especially with the key imprint deception.

We set off with Mad Dog instinctively taking the lead, heading for the safest route down into the cellar.

CHAPTER EIGHT

'A ninja's spirit is not locked in their body . . .'

Sentries were still patrolling the top of the castle perimeter wall, but they were mostly looking outwards, watching for invaders; they weren't expecting intruders right beneath their feet. We had to pass the sleeping area so we kept tight to the dojo, hidden in the shadows, checking through the window every so often to make sure no one was awake. I could see Toby clearly at the end of a row of about eight Kataki, all lined up on their mattresses, facing the same way. It was as though Raven had them all behaving with military precision, even in their sleep. Without his tough façade, Toby looked his age – a fifteen-year-old boy who should be getting excited about his sixteenth birthday, not acting as second-in-command to a brutal murderer who was threatening to inflict agonising pain on him if he didn't carry out his orders and find the scroll. I was more confused than ever now about who could possibly have broken into Yazuki's safe. Neena caught me looking at Toby and gently took my hand. As she touched me, I heard Yazuki's voice ring out in my head: '*Heart can confuse mind.*' I remembered the bitter lesson I'd learned during my training, when Mad Dog and Neena had tricked me in order to teach me not to let emotion rule my ninja actions. In truth, I had no idea if Toby was on our side or not, and on top of that, Dad had managed to plant a seed of doubt about whether he was even my twin after all.

We moved further along the sleeping block towards the castle. As we left, one small ninja caught my eye. Although the figure was dressed in black from head to toe, exactly like all the others, this one was facing the other way, out of line with the rest and somehow more individual. I chose to believe it was Yazuki, giving me a sign that she was here and all would be well. Whether it was or not, I moved on with renewed courage. I took over the lead from Mad Dog, recalling the map Takumi had shown me. I knew exactly where the cellar could be accessed and which would be the safest route down.

There were three ways into the corridors beneath the castle. Takumi's map had shown all the access points and layout of the basement area. Part was a cellar for food storage – that was under the old castle kitchens, the wing of the building that was most damaged and derelict now. Presumably this was why the Kataki had built their brand new dojo with its shiny, clean kitchen. The second set of stairs would have been the way Neena was brought in, which was the most direct route towards the dojo, through the area where she thought they stored their explosives. I didn't want Neena taking us down that way as I suspected this would be the place where the Kataki would most often visit. From Takumi's map I knew there was one more way. This led down to an area near the dungeons – a line of cells where prisoners would have been kept locked up. This route down was a bit unconventional and I hoped it hadn't been blocked up over the years.

We were heading for the lord of the castle's toilet, a chute from his private quarters where all human waste used to pass – into the cellar and into special barrels that would be shipped out by servants or slaves or even prisoners on 'foul' duties. I remembered this from one of my history lessons – a thought which momentarily transported me back to my GCSEs, or rather to the lack of revision I was managing to do up here in Kielder. But there was nothing I could do about that right now, except recall more details about history's toilets – how all the other people who lived within the castle walls would have used outdoor trenches that would be filled in with soil once they were full, but that royalty and important rulers had always had better service when it came to ablutions. I was very grateful for that, as I led the others silently in through the derelict castle walls to the room that was once the lord of the castle's lavatory.

Half the ceiling was missing and through the cracks we could see that most of the walls on the floor above had disintegrated as well. Ivy was growing thick and healthy down the insides of what was left of the building. We'd have to be careful not to disturb anything: with their sharp ninjutsu-trained vision, Raven and the Kataki would be sure to notice if we accidentally pulled any ivy out of place.

Mad Dog looked at me as if to ask why we were here. But I'd already spotted it. In the corner was a rough circular hole that led down to the dungeons. I beckoned for Mad Dog and Neena to follow me over. There was some ivy growing down one side, but I thought we'd be able to slip through the hole without damaging it. I knelt down and leant in, wondering for a moment just what had passed through here before me. But it must have been last used as a toilet centuries ago and the wind and rain had cleaned it as nature had taken over, planting moss and other fine shrubs into the cracks between the stonework. It was dark in the dungeon below, but as I listened, I could hear someone coughing some way away. It felt safe to enter, so I pulled my head back out, gave a quick nod to the others and dropped my feet into the hole, feeling for footholds in the uneven stone wall that ran down to the dungeon floor. The stonework was so rough that it was easy to find something to grip on to – even for Neena who wasn't usually very good with climbing.

When the three of us were safely in the darkness of the dungeon, I signalled for us to all crouch down and close our eyes, to accustom them to the gloom. After about thirty seconds, I opened my eyes and could just make out the corridor, lit partially by moonlight coming in through the hole we'd climbed through and partly by a flaming torch which was mounted on the wall ahead.

We started our journey in a clockwise direction, Neena

leading us towards the area where she'd seen the explosives. We'd hardly gone any distance at all when I saw a stack of something familiar. Explosives, just as I'd seen in the disused tube tunnels beneath Camden underground. So they were definitely planning to blow something up. Next to the explosives there was something I hadn't expected – a pile of ninja wings with body harnesses. But these had been adapted to hold devices that were metal and round and looked like empty bomb shells. There were leather straps that would hang down under the flying ninja, holding the shell, then a simple metal peg keeping the leather thongs together which, when pulled out, would release the straps to let the bomb fall. It looked like the Kataki were planning an aerial strike, which made sense of all the flying training we'd seen.

To one side of the ninja wings, there was a small door that had been left open. I crouched down and peered in, making sure there was no one lurking on the other side. The door led to quite a large room with a low ceiling that ran under the main castle building. It had probably been used for storage – there were old wooden wine racks on the walls, some even with dusty old bottles still in them. But whatever its purpose had been in the past, this room was now definitely used for something more sinister. There was a low table in the middle with a three-dimensional model of Kielder reservoir and the landscape that surrounded it. Little figures of Kataki with wings were lined up along the table. The walls of the room were covered with what looked like mathematical equations scribbled in black ink. There were also pictures of World War Two fighter planes, bombs, buildings that had been devastated by explosions, and areas that were flooded, including images of floating dead bodies and animals. I shuddered. This looked like a wartime campaign room – one that belonged to a dictator with a really warped mind. Raven, no doubt – with a fair amount of Mr Bell thrown in. There was one big cross-section drawing and I beckoned for the others to come in.

'What is it?' Mad Dog whispered.

'Kielder dam wall,' I answered. 'From all these equations, it looks like they're calculating how to blow it up.'

Neena gasped. 'Several hundred families live in that valley,' she whispered. 'If they destroy the dam wall, all the reservoir water will flood out and hundreds of people could drown.'

'Yes,' I answered. 'Their houses will be swept away, to say nothing of all the livestock that'll be drowned and communities devastated.'

'Why would anyone do that?'

'That's what we need to find out.'

'We have to stop them!' said Mad Dog, horrified.

On the far side of the room was a pile of clothes. I went over to check them out, taking great care to pick them up and put them back exactly as I'd found them. They were the uniforms of Kielder reservoir's emergency repair workers. There were fluorescent jackets with logos on and next to the clothes were two machines – waist-height cylinders with handles and a metal point at the bottom.

'Those are Kangas,' Neena whispered. 'They're drills –

exactly like the ones they're using to dig up our road!'

'Hattie, we should be moving,' whispered Mad Dog.

Neena and I followed him back out into the corridor. I made one last mental note of everything in the room, including some detailed drawings of enormous hang-gliding wings, presumably for Raven, since they had feathers sketched on them.

Back in the corridor, we carried on round – next passing two Kielder reservoir vans. I paused and checked them over. They looked like they'd recently been in service.

'The Kataki must have infiltrators in high places if they can get their hands on this kind of thing,' I whispered. The vehicles were right by the door the Kataki had put in to connect the castle dungeons to the massive water overspill tunnel that led down from Kielder reservoir. It was a much bigger door than I'd imagined and they'd done a good job installing it, which was just as well – because if water ever surged along that pipe and came in through the doorway, it would destroy everything down here. On our side of the door there was a huge metal bar right across the wood that was held in place by massive hooks, set deep in concrete in the stonework. I guessed the vehicles had been driven up the spill pipe and brought in this way.

Then I saw something that froze my heart. Mad Dog saw it too. I heard Neena gasp.

'A coffin?' she whispered.

Mad Dog joined us, staring at the roughly hewn wooden box. My head was spinning because daubed in white paint on the side were the two words: *Hattori Hachi . . .*

'That's a little premature, isn't it?' Mad Dog muttered. I was trying to keep calm, but my heart was racing and I could feel my palms were ringing wet again.

'Why would they have that here?' said Neena, panicking.

'They don't know where the scroll is and my guess is that Raven is worried I might still become the Golden Child. If he finds the dagger and kills me with it, perhaps he has to transport my body back to Japan to prove I'm dead.' I could feel myself getting short of breath as I said the words. Suddenly the threat of this mysterious dagger felt a lot more real.

'No, no, no, it's all too terrifying!' Neena gasped, her voice getting higher by the second.

'Not at all,' I said, wiping my hands on my trousers. I took a deep breath and walked on past. 'If I want to avoid ending up in that, we'd better get on with the job in hand.' I wasn't going to let some stupid wooden box scare me.

There was a cough up ahead – like the sound of a person who'd been in the cold and damp for too long. I held my arm up to stop the others while I pulled down my hood to cover my face. I took Dad's climbing crampon from my pocket and started to climb up the wall. Although all the walls were built of stone, there was enough ivy growing down from above, through the gaps in the crumbling stonework, for me to be able to get a grip with one hand and use the climbing crampon in the other. I moved silently across the ceiling for a better look.

Up ahead, I could just make out the iron bars of several prison cells. They were like cages, four of them in a row. A figure was sitting in the cell furthest away, hunched up on the floor. But between him and me was a guard with a blue belt; he was looking at some drawings with someone I couldn't mistake. Mr Bell. I looked back towards the others and was surprised to see Mad Dog right beside me. He'd used Dad's other climbing crampon to follow me. He'd seen the prisoner as well. I took Bushi and Akira from my pocket and felt around for the paper Takumi had given me. I tore off two tiny pieces and put one in each of their mouths. I stroked each of their heads to let them know they were on a mission, pointed, and sent them down the ivy to the floor and off in Mr Bell's direction, hoping he'd recognise them as ninja weapons and go after them, thinking they might be bringing messages from me to his prisoner. I had to trust they'd outrun him and keep enough distance so he couldn't injure them. They knew he was the enemy, that was for sure. I saw the fur on both their necks rise up as they approached him. They were smarter than I could ever have hoped, going the long way round and coming at him from a different direction so he didn't even glance back towards me. Instead, he grabbed a candle and snapped at the guard, 'Be extra vigilant – make sure no one comes down here!' He rushed off after them.

That instruction suited us perfectly. There were three directions to approach the cell – the way Mr Bell had shot off round the dungeon corridor, the way we were coming from, and also another tunnel that ran diagonally under the castle grounds. Which was the guard supposed to watch? Mad Dog provided a solution for him, disappearing across the ceiling, still using his crampon like a climbing claw, making his way into the diagonal tunnel. When he was a safe distance away, he made a quiet shuffling noise. The guard was on his feet in moments, saying, 'Who's there?' as though any enemy was about to reply, '*Oh hi, only me, I've come to attack you, if that's okay?*' Anyway, Mad Dog's little interruption was enough to take the guard off up the tunnel to see what was going on. Neena instinctively took a lookout position where she could see all three tunnels and I dropped down to the floor and ran along to the end cell where the coughing prisoner was huddled up against the bars.

'I'm a friend,' I whispered, 'I don't have much time.'

He swallowed then coughed and wet his lips, like he was having trouble speaking. Eventually, to my amazement, he croaked, 'Is it Hattie?' He turned his head and I nearly screamed. He had no eyes – there was just scar tissue, sunken into his skull in the hollows where his eyeballs had once been. For the second time in less than ten minutes, my palms began to sweat and my heart raced.

'Do I know you?' I whispered. 'How do you know my name?'

'I was a friend of your great-grandfather, Jacko,' he replied, sounding like he hadn't spoken in a long time. 'We both grew up in the tiny village that's now sunken in Kielder reservoir. You can easily check me out – my name's Ridley.'

'You knew my great-granddad all those years ago?'

'I was his apprentice.' That made sense. Ridley looked about seventy, the age my grandparents would have been if they'd lived.

'So you knew Dad too? He's here – they locked us in the tower . . .'

'Yes, I heard. And yes, Hattie, I knew your father when he was a child. Now listen, because we might be interrupted any second.' I crouched down right beside him so he could talk as quietly as possible. He reached through the bars and held my arm as he whispered into my ear. What he said was a total surprise to me. 'Your great-granddad Jacko was a Prisoner of War during World War Two, kept hostage by the Japanese. He escaped, thanks to a Japanese family who helped him. In return, he was asked to smuggle a very special dagger out of the country. The Americans had dropped the first atomic bomb – there was such devastation and it looked as though they might occupy the country. This Japanese family wanted the dagger taken as far away as possible for safe-keeping, in case another bomb was dropped, which in fact it was.'

'The legendary Diamond Dagger?' I asked and he nodded. 'Buried somewhere here in Kielder?'

'Or so Raven believes,' he replied. 'Your great-grandfather and I worked together on this dam with many other residents of our village which was evacuated in order to flood the area.'

'In the late 1970s? When Dad was still a boy – that's when you knew him?'

'Yes. One day, Jacko came to me in a terrible state, begging for help. I would have done anything for him – he was like a father to me. He'd been through a really terrible time. It was shortly after his son and daughter-in-law – your grandparents – were killed . . .'

'In a car crash – an accident.'

'So it was reported.'

'You think they were murdered?'

'Jacko told me bad people were coming after him for the dagger. Your grandparents had been guarding it for him. He got it back from them, but then their house was ransacked and they mysteriously died. Their car was smashed into by a train on a level crossing – though it's possible they were already dead before the accident. Police thought their house was broken into by burglars who knew the owners had just been killed, but nothing was taken. Jacko was convinced the intruders were only after the dagger.' Ridley paused. His whole body trembled. 'Beware of this dagger, Hattie. It's one of the most beautiful things I ever laid my eyes on – when I still had my eyes to see with. Diamonds the size of peas set into it and . . .' he trailed off. 'What is written on the handle, in ancient Japanese, Raven would kill to know. Jacko pleaded with me to take it and look after it for him.'

'Did you?' There was a noise along the corridor and Ridley grabbed my arm.

'You must leave . . .' he whispered, afraid now.

'It's okay, there's time, tell me everything,' I urged him.

'Stories of what the dagger is capable of and who it has killed are legendary,' he continued, talking faster and keeping his voice to a tiny whisper. 'I never got to see what was inscribed on the handle because, as Jacko handed it to me, this terrifying bird-man swooped down and clawed out my eyes.' Now it was my turn to shudder, but Ridley kept talking. 'Don't waste time feeling sorry for me, this happened a long time ago. You must find the dagger, Hattie – it's hewn from the strongest, brightest metal with a blade that will cut through bricks as though they were butter.'

'Where is it, do you know?'

'Jacko tore it from my hands and ran off with it while I fought Raven and stopped him from following. What Raven has never known, is that before he attacked me – while I could still see – Jacko showed me a riddle of where he thought he might hide the dagger, in case I wasn't able to help him. That riddle was on the postcard I sent you. I don't know if that's where he hid it, but it's the only lead I have to help you with. Out loud, Jacko shouted that he would bury the dagger in concrete so no one could ever find it. That's what he wanted Raven to hear. The cement for the dam wall was being poured at that time. It took ten days and this is why Raven believes the dagger is embedded inside.'

'And that's why he's going to blow it up?'

Ridley nodded.

'But that's impossible,' I whispered. 'They'll never find it, surely – that's like looking for a needle in a haystack.'

'Raven has the exact co-ordinates of where the concrete was poured the day Jacko took the dagger. The explosions he's planning, the size of the bombs, everything's calculated to break down the wall exactly to that point.'

'But it isn't there? Is that what you're saying?'

'I don't know, I only know the riddle that I sent to you on the postcard. Raven has tried to torture me to find out what I know, but I have never spoken of it to anyone. In fact, I've never spoken to Raven at all while he's kept me prisoner all these years.'

'How did you manage to write and send a postcard?' I whispered. I didn't know quite how to broach the subject of him being blind. Before he could answer, Neena suddenly appeared, waving frantically. I could hear footsteps a long way off, but they were coming towards us.

'Go back, put your leg irons back on!' I hissed at her. 'Hurry, I'll follow!'

'Hattie . . .' She didn't want to leave without me, but the footsteps were getting louder.

'Go Neena! It's the best thing you can do!' She turned and ran back towards the hole we'd climbed down through.

'There's a guard on our side,' Ridley said. 'He's been here a year, gaining the Kataki's trust. Only in the last week has he let me know he's an infiltrator. He helped me get the postcard to you. That's why he's keeping his distance now. If you're discovered down here he'll pay for it, maybe with his life.'

'Who is he? Do you have any idea?'

'He has a Yorkshire accent, probably from the east of the county, but I've never touched his face, so I can't describe him.'

'And Great-granddad Jacko? What happened to him?'

'I never saw him again. No one did. The dagger was never found. The dam was finished and the reservoir filled and our village became the sunken ghost town it is today. I know you're special, Hattie, that your family is the most highly regarded in Japan. Jacko insisted that if anything happened to him, I should make contact with the Hattoris

141

because they were the only people who could be trusted to take charge of this terrifying weapon. It took sixteen years before I was able to engineer your father's visit to your mother's family. I was living in a home – which I now know had been chosen by Raven and filled with people keeping watch on me. I was traumatised and mute after the shock of Raven's attack. But one day I woke up and I could speak again. I've never told anyone, Hattie. I would just whisper to myself every day to practise using my voice. As far as Raven knows, I'm still mute now. But with that change came the realisation that I must do something to avenge your great-grandfather's death. In secret, I sent word to your dad – about to set off on his travels as a twenty-five-year-old man. I had visitors who were still in touch with him. They would come and tell me news of our community. Still I pretended to be mute, not wanting Raven to know my voice had come back. But I could write, so with one of them helping, I secretly sent a letter to your father saying that he was to visit the Hattoris as he passed through Japan. The rest is history.'

'Dad knows about the dagger?'

'No. Raven must have suspected me of communicating with someone and I was taken out of the home and imprisoned, then moved from camp to camp for years. I never got to tell your father any more of the story.'

The footsteps were dangerously close now and Mad Dog appeared, looking anxious.

'I've thought about that riddle every day of my life, Hattie, and am still no nearer to solving where your great-granddad hid the dagger. All I can think is this . . .'

Ridley spoke so softly I wasn't sure I'd even heard. But there was no time to ask him to repeat it. Mad Dog grabbed my arm and dragged me away. We shot into the shadows and Mad Dog legged it back along the corridor. I paused long enough to look back, hiding behind some ivy. Mr Bell arrived first, followed by at least six other Kataki, all surrounding Raven, like they were his armed guards. The reason they'd taken so long to get to us must have been because Raven was so unstable on his feet. He limped as he walked and it looked as though his left leg was very painful. Close up, I could see he was much older than I expected – maybe in his seventies. But he was obviously a proud man, refusing help from any of his guards.

I was fixed to the spot, looking at this evil man who had clawed out Ridley's eyes and kept him locked up in this hell hole for years. Raven hobbled up to Ridley's cell and spoke in a terrifying voice with a heavy Japanese accent.

'Rats running messages to you, yes?' I desperately hoped he'd only heard that Bushi and Akira had been running around and hadn't actually got his hands on them. 'So you are able to write and communicate?!' This was further proof to me that Raven was deranged – no one in their right mind could possibly think Ridley could read and write messages on tiny pieces of paper. Raven snapped his fingers and Mr Bell stepped forward, handing a pen and paper to Raven, which Raven then pushed into Ridley's hands. 'So go on – show me how you write!' he snarled.

It was now that I got my first good look at Raven's face. I knew Mad Dog would be worried sick, but I couldn't move. My head was spinning and the noise in my ears was deafening me. I knew it wasn't real noise I could hear; it was the sounds that had haunted me ever since my mind-merge with Suzi. Screaming, shouting, sirens, but most of all this sickening flapping sound, accompanied by the smell of burning flesh. My mind's eye saw the big black wings, burning now as, in my head, Raven flapped above me, his hair on fire, his face melting all down one side, his skin peeling from his cheekbone. He was screaming, just as he screamed now to Ridley:

'I WILL KNOW THE TRUTH! YOU WILL ANSWER ME!'

I snapped out of my memory as Mr Bell unlocked the cell door and pulled Ridley to his feet. Raven pushed his way in, jabbing his vicious, shiny claw-like tool into Ridley's chest. His face was horribly scarred all down the left side and his ear was missing. He looked even more terrifying close up than in the air, flying. I was sick with fear about what he was going to do to Ridley, but there was no way I could help. While everyone's attention was on the poor blind man, I backed down the tunnel to find Mad Dog.

Mad Dog grabbed me and pushed me up through the hole. I scrambled onto the ground above and reached back in to help him climb up. We just looked at each other, choked, as we heard Ridley's cries of agony, echoing along the tunnel.

CHAPTER NINE

'Pursue personal harmony in the total scheme of things.'

Getting back to our prison tower was relatively easy and I hoped Neena's journey to the kitchen had been as swift. Once Raven started torturing Ridley, every guard was distracted for a few minutes by the noise. Dawn was breaking as Mad Dog and I ran to the tower and climbed as far as we could up the underside of the stone spiral staircase, then waited until the guard ran down a few steps to see whether he was needed in the dungeon. The two of us slid unseen up on to the staircase above the guard and ran to the door. It unlocked more easily than before and we flew in, re-locked it and slipped effortlessly into our beds, which Dad had prepared by unrolling the mattresses as he heard us come in. None of us spoke for several minutes. We heard our guard return and I sensed him coming to the door to look through and check on us. Then he moved away. Nothing happened for a while and, eventually, it felt safe to pretend all the noise had woken us up.

I shifted in my bed and rolled over to look at Dad. He stared back, concerned. *'You okay?'* he mouthed. I nodded, wondering where on earth to start. I wanted to tell him about his family history and Ridley's involvement in bringing the Jacksons and the Hattoris together. I'd had enough of hiding things from him and decided that being honest and asking him to help me understand everything was by far the best option.

However, it was almost more than I could bear, as I started to tell Dad how his parents may not have died in an accident, but been murdered. I didn't know how much the poor man could take in on one short out-of-town trip. But actually, he took it remarkably well. He listened attentively and asked questions as I filled him in on everything about Ridley being a prisoner in the dungeon and all he'd told me about the dagger and how Jacko had brought it to England after he escaped from Japan. Actually, it was Mad Dog who seemed to find the story most overwhelming.

'That blind man sent your dad to meet your mum?'

'Yes,' I told him for the third time.

'I remember,' Dad said. 'I got his strange letter – big writing, as though a child had written it. Ridley's cousin brought it to me just before I went travelling. I had no reason to believe it wasn't from him. We all knew he'd lost his sight, but no one had actually seen him since it had happened. We were just told it was an industrial accident. So yes, it was all because of Ridley that I searched out the Hattoris when I was passing through Japan.'

Mad Dog was still having trouble processing everything. 'So if it wasn't for this dagger and Raven, then you wouldn't have met Hattie's mum and Hattie might never have been born?'

'I guess not,' Dad said.

'So something good has come out of all this evil?'

'Life's like that,' Dad continued. 'It's worth remembering, nothing's ever black and white and the greatest things in life can evolve from the most dire of situations.'

Then he paused and I knew the awfulness of Ridley's situation had finally hit him. 'What can we do to help Ridley?' he whispered. 'He's a lovely man – he was always laughing and so kind. He should never have been dragged into this nightmare . . .'

'We'll help him,' I said, 'as soon as we can.' I carried on telling Dad what we'd seen in the dungeons – all the explosives, the campaign room, the two vehicles and the emergency services uniforms, though I didn't tell him about the coffin with my name on it. When I mentioned the calculations for blowing up the dam wall, he sighed heavily.

'There's going to be carnage, that's for sure,' he said, then added, *'Only the dead have seen the last of war*, that's written up in the Imperial War Museum. My granddad Jacko took me there every year when I was small – we'd come down on the train, even after your granddad and granny died. Jacko said you had to see the world to discover yourself and to see all the good of humanity and that essentially we're all the same, regardless of race, colour, creed, religion —'

'So, this message from Ridley?' I interrupted.

'He wanted me to meet the Hattoris.'

'Did he say why?'

'No, not really. I thought maybe Granddad Jacko knew them. But when I got there, it turned out he didn't. They didn't know what I was on about. Ridley said to phone him once I'd made contact with them because he had a message for them from my granddad.'

'But Ridley went missing before he could give you the message?'

'Yes. And if I had been given a message for the Hattoris, I'd probably know a lot more about all this ninjutsu business,' he said. 'I did call him. He just never answered. I only found out when I got back two years later – married to your mum with you as a tiny baby – that Ridley had disappeared. It was mid-winter and there was deep snow. His family had been told he'd wandered off from the home and never come back. They thought he'd died of exposure.'

'But his body was never found. Didn't anyone think it was odd, that Great-granddad Jacko and Ridley both went missing?' I asked.

'People go missing all the time.'

'They don't just evaporate into thin air!'

'They do up on the moors in the middle of winter. They perish and their bodies are never found. And there were so many years between them disappearing – why would anyone link them?'

Mad Dog suddenly interrupted. 'They're doing it again!' He'd been keeping watch out of the east window.

We went to look. Even though it was hardly light, the Kataki were retrieving round bomb shells from the lake and loading them into a van as though to recycle them for another round of practice bomb drops.

'What's Raven up to?' Mad Dog said.

'I wish I knew,' I answered.

'The bouncing bomb,' Dad suddenly announced. 'He's been watching that *Dam Busters* film. You remember, Hattie – I must have seen it a dozen times.'

'I remember you watching it, but I never have.'

'Fantastic film. Great invention – Barnes-Wallis, genius of a man. Came up with a bomb that would detonate at a certain depth to blow up a dam wall. But it had to explode right next to the concrete to have the power to break it. Even a metre away wouldn't do. They couldn't drop bombs vertically from moving planes with that kind of accuracy, so Barnes-Wallis took the principle of stones skimming across the water and applied it to dropping bombs.'

'The pilots flew really low, didn't they?' Mad Dog said. 'I saw that film, years ago.'

'Yes, as the bombs dropped, they needed to be travelling with forward momentum. When they hit the water, they bounced – like skimming stones,' said Dad, his eyes shining now. 'I bet that's exactly what they're up to here! Barnes-Wallis did the maths, quite brilliant, so the bombs would slow down and when they came to the dam wall, they would stop and gently sink until, at a precise depth – *boom!*' He clapped his hands and we both jumped. 'The hydrostatic pistols exploded the charges just where they wanted and blew the dam sky high. Water flooded out, destroyed everything in its path – mainly the Germans' factories in the flood-plain of the reservoir, the Ruhr valley, which was their main ball bearing production area. You can't make any fighting equipment without ball bearings, so that air strike practically won us the war. Turned the tide anyway – well, that and the atomic bomb, which was really what ended everything.'

'Didn't people drown when they blew up the dam walls?' I asked, thinking this didn't sound so great for the Germans.

Dad paused. 'It was war,' he said. 'Things were different then.'

'Don't see how,' I answered. 'Isn't that what people always say? Surely if we want the world to change, we have to be moral and responsible even in war.'

'Hattie, you weren't there,' he said. 'It's much more complicated than that.' He was using the deep voice he always adopted when he didn't want me answering back.

'Okay,' said Mad Dog. 'If the bombs have to slide down hard against the dam wall, why don't the Kataki just walk up there and drop them by hand?'

'Because less than a second from letting go, the dam wall will blow sky high and they'd be blown to pieces with it,' I answered, thinking it was pretty obvious. 'Or drowned, depending how the wall breaks down and the water floods out.'

'Good point,' Mad Dog replied.

'I used to know all the families living on the flood-plain

– they could still be there,' Dad said. 'In Falstone, Yarrow, Stannesburn . . . If that reservoir goes, they'll be drowned and, as the water surges, it'll bring down the rest of the dam wall, causing it to crumble into the valley below, along with the concrete valve tower which will be knocked over by the force of the water.'

'Look at him,' Mad Dog interrupted. He was watching through the window as Raven swooped and soared, attacking his own men. 'The man's possessed.'

'If he's this vicious to his own side . . .' Dad said.

'Yes, who'd want to be his enemy,' I replied. '*To fight the enemy, attack his weakest points*. He's a bully and that means, deep down, he's terrified.'

'So why the vehicles and the concrete breakers with reservoir workers' clothes in the basement?' Mad Dog asked, partly to himself and partly to anyone who might have an answer.

I'd been thinking about this ever since we'd seen those things in the dungeon. 'They'll fly over the reservoir, drop their bombs and fly on, landing inside the castle,' I replied. 'Then they'll put on their emergency service outfits, drive the vans back up to the dam wall and, while the real emergency services are trying to rescue people on the flood-plain, the Kataki will break up the concrete to exactly where they believe the dagger is buried.'

'It feels so imprecise, though,' Mad Dog said. 'That dagger could be anywhere. Even if they manage to bomb within centimetres of where it's supposed to be buried, aren't they worried they'll damage or destroy this precious dagger?'

'It's supposed to be indestructible – guess they're banking on that,' I said.

'No, you're right, Mad Dog,' Dad added. 'Raven thinks it's rational, but his plan's completely flawed. It's often the case with megalomaniacs. They get what they think is a brilliant plan that somehow makes them feel superhuman – and all their minions are so terrified of disagreeing, no one argues or points out the obvious and the tyrant's ego just gets bigger and bigger and all logic and rational thinking goes right out the window.'

'It's all irrelevant anyway because the dagger's probably not even in the dam wall at all,' I said. 'Ridley's pretty sure that was just Jacko sending them off in the wrong direction.'

'Won't the castle be devastated as well?' asked Mad Dog. 'When the dam wall goes?'

Dad already had that worked out. 'We're not in the flood-plain here,' he said. 'We're just on the path of the overspill water tunnel.'

'But Takumi's house is,' I said. 'If Takumi's in there when the water hits, he'll never get out alive.'

We were interrupted by a scream and several sets of feet hurrying up the spiral stairs. 'That's Neena!' I said, rushing to the door. There was another shout, but this time Neena put words to it.

'Stop HURTING me!' she yelled. 'What's happened to you, Toby – why are you so violent all the time?'

A key turned in the lock and the door flew wide open and Toby hurled Neena in to join us. I saw straight away she didn't have her leg irons on. She just shook her head and I guessed she hadn't got back to the dojo quickly enough. Toby stood there with Mr Bell and two Kataki guards, the four of them filling the doorway, looking pretty scary.

'We know you've been creeping around,' Toby said, glaring at Neena then at me. 'Our little cook hid from us for a while, but no one escapes. We know you visited Ridley, she told us.'

Neena shook her head and I knew she hadn't told them anything. Toby was just trying to trick us.

He carried on, 'Raven's on his way and he's very unhappy, so if I were you, I'd say right now what Ridley told you. Where's the dagger?'

I wondered whether Toby would have talked differently to us if Mr Bell and the two guards hadn't been there. I felt very strongly that his words and actions were designed to prove to the Kataki that he was one of them. On the other hand, he didn't have to hurt Neena like he had. Her hand was bleeding from where he had thrown her on to the rough stone floor.

There was the sound of uneven footsteps on the staircase and then Raven pushed his way into the room. We were all sitting on the floor now so, even though he wasn't a big man, it felt like he was towering over us, twice as fearsome and ugly this close up, with what appeared to be his new, even bigger set of huge black wings. They were exactly like the drawings I'd seen in his campaign room, which made me think he was fast building up to his mission. Raven obviously thought his new wings would make him more scary – and he was right. He puffed them up just enough so they doubled his size. Dad immediately sprang to his feet while Neena took hold of my hand. I could feel she was shaking. What was so scary about Raven this close up was that his eyes darted around, like a bird about to attack and peck your eyeballs.

Raven looked at each of us in turn, his sharp, beady stare full of hatred and anger. 'You were there, talking to him. That much we got out of him.' I knew he could be lying, using a trick to get us to admit what he suspected. 'Ridley always acted mute, even during our interrogations, but this time you heard him screaming just like we all did. Cried like a baby and admitted everything. And all because Mr Bell heard your whispers along the corridor. Smart, young Hattori Hachi, but just not smart enough.'

I hoped to goodness Ridley was still alive and felt pretty sure he wouldn't have told Raven anything about our conversation.

'Less than twenty-four hours till your birthday,' Raven continued. 'A big problem for us if we don't find the scroll and the dagger.'

So they definitely didn't have the scroll – that made me feel a little relieved, at least.

'What makes you think you're any more entitled to the Hattori wealth than anyone else?' I suddenly said, without even meaning to open my mouth. I was just fed up with Raven's bullying. Neena dug her nails in, terrified that I was answering him back but actually I knew that, for now at least, I was safe. If I did manage to sign the scroll and inherit the

Hattori wealth and power, then Raven needed the Diamond Dagger to kill me, which I knew for sure he didn't have. So this really was my one chance to answer back – to see if I could deduce any more about Raven and how to defeat him. I carried on. 'I understand the history, Raven – but I don't understand why the dagger is so important to you.' I needed to hear him say it.

He laughed. 'You will when you feel the cold blade slice across your throat,' he replied. 'Tell us where it is and we will release the others. And tell us where you have hidden the scroll, otherwise we will kill them one at a time in front of you now.'

I looked straight at Toby. Did he know who had taken the scroll? He wasn't about to give anything away.

'What did that blind fool tell you?' Raven repeated. 'Tell me, or I will score your flesh like an orange and peel back your skin strip by strip.' He held up his right arm and his ninja jacket sleeve fell back, revealing a terrifying metal claw. Dad bristled. Raven stepped towards me, menacing, and looking for all the world as though he really meant to inflict pain.

Toby was the next person to move, stepping in and shouting in my face, 'How did you get out? Show me, do you have a key?'

I didn't say anything and I didn't flinch. I just kept sitting still, until Toby grabbed me and pulled me to my feet, already feeling through my pockets. He pulled out Dad's crampon. Then he found the key. I'd had no way of hiding any of it in this empty prison room. He took Takumi's paper and all the tools and plant remedies and stuffed everything into his own pockets. The only thing he missed was Takumi's pen, which I'd hidden in a secret pouch in my trousers. Toby growled and his eyes burnt, as though they were about to turn red again. His shadow panther animus started forming on the wall as Raven turned and stepped aggressively towards the guard who should have stopped us escaping.

'You FOOL!' he screamed and pushed the guard off-balance, sending him over the banister, tumbling down the centre of the spiral stairwell. There were screams and an awful noise of cracking bones as the guard's body crashed to the bottom.

Raven turned back into the room. 'Deal with them!' he screamed at Toby, whose eyes were even more on fire now. Toby honed in on me with Ridley's postcard in his hand. Dad and Mad Dog looked at each other in a way that worried me. If Toby came any closer, I feared they were both going to attack him. Toby was terrifying, I have to admit, but I felt sure I knew what he was doing – bullying me to deflect Raven, and simply trying to get me to tell them what they needed to know. But he had to do it in a realistic way.

I quickly considered my options – I could fight Toby, but I couldn't fight off Raven, Mr Bell and the other guards as well. Even with Mad Dog using his best ninja skills, we'd be overpowered. Dad would give his all, and Neena too, but they'd all be dead in seconds and I'd be kept alive just long enough for Raven and Mr Bell to make me help them find the Diamond Dagger so they could kill me in a slow, agonising way.

Still Toby kept coming and now two more Kataki came up

the stairs and into the room, both with swords. They pushed all of us on to our knees and held their deadly weapons against our necks as Toby thrust the postcard in my face.

'What did Ridley tell you?!' he roared, striking me with a huge hand that felt like a big cat's paw. Well, that was it.

'ENOUGH!' yelled Dad, and I could see he was about to explode with rage. 'I don't know who you think you are Toby, but you're nothing but a BULLY!'

Toby snarled and all the Kataki raised their swords. A fight wasn't going to help anyone – least of all the people who were going to drown if Raven blew up the reservoir. I had to stop them.

'Tower,' I announced in a very clear voice. 'Ridley said tower.'

Everyone turned to look at me.

'He thought the message had something to do with a tower, that's what he told me.'

It was all that was needed to diffuse the situation and suddenly the Kataki lowered their swords and stepped back as Raven moved towards me.

'I'll tell you everything I know,' I said. 'Please don't hurt the others.' I got up and held out my hand to Toby for the card. I took it to Raven. 'Okay, from what I can see . . .' I pointed to the letters on the card:

T

D

D

T

'The two *T*s, written vertically, with two *D*s in the middle signify that the Diamond Dagger – or *DD* – is hidden in a tower, represented by the two *T*s. My only guess about *wage war* is that my great-grandfather, Jacko, wanted people to know the dagger is precious enough for people to start a major war over it. Or to torture people, or to brutalise or murder,' I said, looking icily at Raven, then Toby. 'And I can assure you that's all I know for now. I have no idea who *Tanil* is, but if you give me some time, maybe I can work that out as well. But, if you lay one finger on my father, my friends, or on me, I will die attempting to kill every one of you before I ever help you find the dagger. As for the scroll, someone took it. I'm sure you've had people scouring our home in Camden for it. But it's not there and I don't know where it is. My guess is that it will turn up, after being kept somewhere secure, so it can be brought safely to me, maybe by my mother, or maybe my *sensei-san* so you'd better keep me alive, or you may never see that again either.'

I couldn't believe I'd said all this with such authority. I had no idea whether me bluffing like this would work. For all I knew, the Kataki might actually have had the scroll. But Raven, despite his brutality, was a bit of a sucker for straight talk. He snatched the postcard off me and swooped out, followed by his minions. Just Toby was left, glaring at us all, and a new guard who was already in place with his red belt, standing by the door.

'The dagger is right here, Toby, under your nose,' I told him. 'Somewhere in this tower. I hope that, if you find it, you will choose to do the right thing.'

Toby reached in his pocket and took out something wrapped in a cloth, about the size of a hot dog.

'You're completely screwed,' he said. 'Your pathetic little rats as well. He threw down the package and it landed with a dull thud. 'That's what happens when you get others to do your dirty work.' With that, Toby left.

I looked at the package feeling as sick as anything. They must have caught either Bushi or Akira – or both. The new guard slammed the door shut and locked it. Then we heard more people climbing the stairs with a lot of crashing and thumping. Mad Dog crossed to the door to look into the stairwell.

'They're boarding us up,' he said. 'So much for Toby being on our side. We're doomed. They're bringing up a massive piece of wood . . . They're boarding up the door, Hattie!'

On the other side of the door, the Kataki were banging enormous nails into the sheet of wood, attaching it to the door frame and completely blocking any chance of an exit that way.

'What are we going to do, Hattie?!' Mad Dog said, pacing the room and trying to think of something.

He was panicking, but I didn't answer. I knelt down and just stared at the package on the floor, trying not to cry at the thought of Bushi or Akira – or both – suffering at the hands of the Kataki.

CHAPTER TEN

'Let the wind and rain protect you; darkness is your greatest friend.'

The others watched in silence as I picked up the cold little body wrapped in Toby's bundle. I could feel the lifeless corpse and even the tiny bones. The sun was streaming in now as Neena spoke gently to me.

'Do you want me to look and see which one it is?' I shook my head and unwrapped the soft cloth. Inside was another cloth tied with string and I wondered what exactly Toby had done to my poor rats that needed string to hold them together. But as I untied it, I was surprised to find a sock inside. The bones were more evident now – but I could feel they were a bit loose as well. Then I realised this sock was familiar . . .

'Look!' I whispered. 'Neena – it's my sock!' There on the ankle, in Neena's tiny, neat embroidery, were the words, *Work Socks*. She came to look.

'How did Toby get hold of that?' she whispered.

'I lent them to Mum!'

Dad joined us, hopeful that maybe this meant Mum wasn't too far away. I shook the sock and out tumbled some dried bones and some paper, wrapped round something hard.

'Those are chicken bones,' Neena whispered, glancing at the door.

'It's okay, they can't see anything, we're completely boarded up,' Mad Dog whispered, coming over to look as well. My heart was racing.

'It's not Bushi or Akira at all!' I unfolded the paper and held out the contents. In my hand was a small hacksaw blade. Yazuki had one just like it and I knew that, although it wasn't very big, it would be super strong and perfect for sawing through the bars of our prison windows.

Dad took it and tried to bend it. 'Exactly what we need,' he said. 'Do you think Toby knew what was in the parcel?'

'I don't know, Dad,' I whispered, pointing to remind him the Kataki were just outside the door. 'Although I really hope he knew, it's possible he killed Bushi or Akira and Mum managed to switch parcels so she could get the blade to us.'

I turned over the paper the blade had been wrapped in. There were drawings on the other side – a cross-section of the reservoir with diagrams and arrows, showing how the Kataki were going to fly over and drop bombs and cause the dam wall to break. Written at the bottom, in Mum's handwriting, were just two words: *Midnight tonight*.

'They're planning their attack for the moment of my birthday,' I said.

The hacksaw blade gave Dad hope. He tried it on one of the window bars. At least with the door boarded up, the guard couldn't see or hear him. But as he sawed, it did make a noise.

'Hold on, Dad,' I whispered. 'The Kataki are outside as well – we can't risk them hearing.'

But nature was once again on our side. Dark clouds were rolling in and the sky was grey and foreboding. Suddenly, a lightning bolt lit up the castle grounds followed by an almighty crack of thunder. The heavens opened and rain flooded down. We could hear Kataki moving around the tower, searching every room for the dagger – floor to ceiling. And there were definitely a couple of ninjas on the roof above us – we could hear them banging and tearing up tiles. But once again, Raven appeared in the clearing below and took the change in weather as his cue to start some more flying training. He was shouting orders, supervising, as in the distance a bright lamp suddenly came on. I could just make out that it was the one I'd seen at the far end of the lake.

'What are they doing?' I exclaimed. 'I told them about the tower!'

'They're not leaving anything to chance,' Dad answered. 'If they don't find the dagger here, they'll blow up the dam wall anyway.'

'The lamp marks the spot,' Mad Dog said. 'That's what they're doing. It's where the bombers have to drop their payload.'

We watched as, below us, other Kataki ran around with giant wings and Mr Bell and three ninjas with green belts carried out the board I'd seen in the campaign room – the model of Kielder reservoir and the hills around it. They put a canopy over it to protect it from the rain which meant we couldn't see any details, but beyond it, we could just make out Mr Bell putting up a wind sock to check wind force and direction for hang-gliding.

'There are only three places they could launch from round here,' Dad said. 'Deadwater Fell to the north in the Kielderhead Nature Reserve. That's about the nearest place. Unless the wind's in the wrong direction – then they'd be better off using Purdom's Pike. Actually, that makes more sense. You can see the reservoir from up there so they'd be able to use the lamp to communicate with the hang-gliders as well as to illuminate the target spot on the lake. But then there's always Berrymoor Edge in the Cheviot Hills, up near the Otterburn army ranges. Very high for launching, which is good, but further away and dangerously close to military land and they won't want to be caught messing around up there. It's used as a bombing range for jets and as a test site for live ammunition.'

'Perhaps that's where they got their explosives from,' Neena said.

'It's all high fences and armed guards,' Dad answered. 'If they've got access up there, they really do have friends in high places.'

I shut my eyes and tried to mind-merge with Raven, to see if I could think like him and work out anything at all about what he was planning. But all I got was a sudden jumbled mess of anger and such frightening dark shapes that I stopped trying. I didn't want to fill my own head with negative thoughts prior to an important mission.

The Kataki started climbing up on to the castle ramparts wearing their wings, jumping off and then plummeting really fast towards the lake, before swooping low to practise dropping their empty bomb cases. The light was shining on and off, marking the target just as Dad predicted. Raven was obsessed, making his warriors practise in these dire conditions, but it suited us perfectly. No one was paying us any attention.

Mad Dog and Dad got a system going, each taking it in turns to saw like crazy while the weather stopped any sound from travelling. The sawing was unbelievably slow. It took forever to even make a tiny groove on the bottom of the end bar, but they weren't going to let that deter them.

'We've got all day,' Dad said. 'We don't want to escape too early anyway. If the attack's not till midnight, we don't want to get out till dark.'

We'd worked out that we'd need to remove at least two bars for the gap to be wide enough for us all to get through. Neena was still very concerned.

'What if they find the Diamond Dagger?' she asked.

'They won't,' I answered.

'But what if they do?' she said again. 'They'll kill you, Hattie. They won't wait or anything – they'll just come after you and that'll be it. Curtains.'

'Thanks for that thought,' I said. 'But I have to sign the

scroll before I inherit the title, so there won't be any immediate danger.'

'Other than them suddenly announcing they've had the scroll all along, then standing over you, making you sign it then killing you, so you'll never be able to help all the people in Japan and around the world who are relying on you.'

'Perhaps you could think of something a bit more cheerful, Neena?' was all I could think to reply, glancing at Dad, knowing he was already right on the edge about me going off fighting.

'Sorry,' Neena muttered, and set about wrapping the chicken bones back in the sock and putting them in one of her pockets.

I glanced out of the window, hoping Bushi and Akira were both okay, then I turned back and said, 'I don't think for a minute the clue means *this* tower by the way. Why would it? Jacko probably never even knew this place existed. I'm pretty sure *tower* is only part of the answer. I think the real clue is in the signature, *Tanil*.'

'We should be able to work it out then,' said Neena. 'Is it an anagram?'

Dad looked up. 'Granddad Jacko was big on crosswords. He loved how words are formed. If he hadn't been drafted into the army to fight in the war, he'd have been a teacher, I'm sure. But the P.O.W. camp killed his spirits. He was always very nervy, especially later on, after . . .' He trailed off and I knew Dad was thinking about his parents' car crash again.

'We have to think clearly and solve this puzzle, Dad,' I

said. 'We mustn't let emotion rule our heads.'

'Has Toby tricked your mum as well?' he replied, off on another tangent. 'Has he convinced her he's your brother?'

'You'll have to ask her,' I said.

'Why did she never mention any of this to me? I mean, why would she let the two of you carry on under this awful misapprehension that your brother wasn't killed when he was a baby and not discuss it with me? If by some unbelievable miracle it did turn out to be true, didn't she think I had a right to know?'

'We'll talk about this, Dad,' I reassured him, 'when we're out of here and back home with Mum. But for now, I really need you to help with this. You're the only one who might be able to work out what Great-granddad Jacko meant. Is *Tanil* an anagram?'

Dad looked away. He was finding it hard to focus and I hoped it meant he was starting to consider whether Toby really was his son. In my mind, although I was still certain Toby was my twin brother, I was now seriously doubting that he was ever going to leave the Kataki.

'Come on, Dad,' I said. 'Tell me more about Great-granddad Jacko – let's try and get inside his head.'

'He'd read the dictionary like it was a story book,' Dad suddenly said. 'Loved how words were formed, always telling me what the roots of words were and how they came about.'

'So is it *Latin*?' Neena asked. 'The anagram? Roots of words mostly come from Latin, and *Tanil* is an anagram of *Latin*. I can't see any other full words it could be, unless

166

Laint is a word, or *Tailn* or *Nailt* – but of course we all know they aren't.'

'Letters mean things in Latin, don't they?' said Mad Dog. 'Like they sometimes have on the telly? At the end of old programmes?'

'Those are numbers,' said Neena. 'Roman numerals like X, V and I – giving the date when a programme was made.'

'So these *T*s and *D*s in a column don't mean something in Latin?' Mad Dog asked.

'It's not to do with the column of letters,' I said. 'It's the *wage war*, he means. He wouldn't write anything as obvious as 'the enemy will wage war to get this' – the *wage war* is what refers to *Tanil* . . . That's the clue.'

None of us had ever learnt Latin at school, so we were no better off. I hoped it would mean something to Dad, that maybe Great-granddad Jacko had taught him some Latin when he was a child. But when I asked him again if this meant anything to him, he just shook his head.

'What else hasn't your mum told me?' he said, in a cheerful way that I knew was him hiding the hurt he was feeling because there was so much she hadn't told him.

'I don't know, Dad,' I replied, in the most controlled voice I could. 'But I'm sure you'll be able to ask her for yourself very soon. If we solve this and get out alive.' I did feel sorry for him, trying to absorb all this ninjutsu information, as well as the truth about his parents' death and being told Toby was his son. I wanted to be kind, but I wished he could just concentrate and help us, because solving this riddle could be a matter of life and death for all of us.

'At the very least I have to get out to see if Mum's got the scroll,' I said. 'If Toby really is one of the Kataki, then I have to sign it and become the Golden Child.'

'Where is your mum?' Dad said, like he hadn't been listening to anything I'd said. 'Is that her there?' He was staring out of the window and, sure enough, a flying Kataki was heading our way. For just a second, even with the full hood, I thought I recognised Mum's eyes. I had no idea what orders her *chunin* had given her, but there was every chance she was very close, especially now we'd had this parcel with the hacksaw wrapped in her sock. I closed my eyes and thought this was a perfect moment to try to mind-merge with her. I put myself out there, hang-gliding, as though I was Mum. In my mind's eye, I looked down on us in our prison cell. But I couldn't feel anything, except a longing to be back in the room with Dad and Mad Dog, to know we were all safe.

'If it's her, I'm sure she wants to be with us as much as we want to be with her,' I said. 'But there's no way she can connect with us. She's undercover and even a look could give her away. The same for Yazuki. We must carry on as though neither of them exists.'

The hang-glider turned and swooped away, heading back to drop their bomb where the light was being shone on the lake. I looked one last time, desperately hoping it was Mum.

'How are you doing with that saw, Mad Dog?' Neena said.

He stepped back so we could all see. 'Quite hard going,'

he answered. He'd still hardly made a mark on the first bar.

'Better try twice as hard then,' I said, with an encouraging smile.

After that, the day seemed to fly by. Although it was hours before we could even think of leaving our cell, this was the last day of me being fifteen and I knew that turning sixteen was going to change my life forever, whatever the outcome. I tried to hold on to every minute but I couldn't slow time down. I should have tried to sleep but my mind was buzzing. I mentally went back over all my training – revisiting the thought processes I'd learned from the five Dans about going into battle. I especially considered the Fifth level – the state of *ku*, which had allowed me to mind-merge so I could overcome Praying Mantis – my Aunt Suzi. I was already aware that the speed we were sawing through the bars would only allow one bar to be removed and the gap would be minuscule. I was the smallest of everyone and I was going to have to force myself out through that hole if it was the last thing I did. No one else would make it. Luckily, none of the others had realised it yet. Dad, for one, would have a fit if he thought I'd be setting off alone to face Raven and stop the bombing of the dam wall. But I was pretty sure that's how it would have to be. I had to be as focused as I'd ever been.

CHAPTER ELEVEN

'Either live in the moment –
or spend a lifetime dying.'

By eight o'clock in the evening, Mad Dog had sawed through the bottom of the first bar, but was still only two-thirds of the way through the top. His hands were red raw. I was bursting with nervous energy and also aware that I needed to keep my muscles loose. And as I wanted to keep Dad's mind focused on positive things, I decided to kill two birds with one stone and get him to help me start my warm-up for tonight's mission.

First, I got Dad acting as a block while I practised my kicks. He was pretty good and threw in a few police training tips as well.

'It's a dirty trick,' he told me, 'but if you're really stuck, go for the groin or the eyes.'

'Like this?' I said and kicked him playfully on the forehead. I didn't want to tell him that I could kill with a single blow and knock someone unconscious with pressure in the right place on their neck.

'No, the eyes,' he said, 'not the forehead,' like I was supposed to give him a real kick and blind him.

'Yeah, thanks Dad,' I said, realising he wasn't really equipped to help me train. 'As a rule, I just mark things through when I'm warming up. I wouldn't want to hurt you.'

Dad went over to the window and took the blade off Mad Dog. 'You help her,' he said.

Even Neena hadn't seen some of what Mad Dog and I could do once we got going. She watched, amazed, as we fought and backflipped and ran up walls and went through all our unarmed combat, as well as our full 'tools and weapons' repertoire – even though we had to mime everything.

'Okay, now for real,' I said. 'Do it, Mad Dog – I need you to.' He went at me with every move he knew – none of it pre-rehearsed like so many of our exercises. He didn't hold back. He knew tonight my life could depend on being sharp and properly warmed-up. He tried to floor me, hit me, trick me and generally show he was a stronger and better fighter. He failed at every point. By now, Dad was watching too, which made Mad Dog try all the harder. We fought on and on till my limbs were crying out to stop. Then I let Mad Dog grab my arm and twist me down and yelled, 'Okay, you win, let go!'

He winked, knowing I'd done this for Dad's benefit.

'Good work, lad,' Dad said. 'But I think she had you in the first three seconds.'

'She certainly did,' said Mad Dog and he looked at me with that twinkle in his eye and I knew he meant that I'd captured his heart the very first time we met.

'They're stopping,' Neena suddenly called out. 'Meal time – yay! Okay, please, please, please eat the soup . . . eat the soup, eat the soup . . .'

'Wish I could have some more of that,' Mad Dog said, taking the hacksaw blade off Dad and getting back down to work. 'You realise they didn't bring us any lunch today?'

'They always have soup at supper time.' Neena grinned. 'Their last meal before their mission. You might have enjoyed it last night, Mad Dog – and you'd enjoy it again now, I'm sure. But in about an hour I guarantee you'd wish you hadn't.'

'What did you do?' I asked, looking out as two Kataki brought the massive pot of soup to where bowls were being handed round.

'The best ninja trick in the book,' Neena smiled. 'Used by Lord Li on the warriors of Nikko, as I recall . . .'

'Laxatives,' I said with an approving smile.

'Lots,' she replied.

Mad Dog laughed. 'That's what you added as we left the kitchen last night?'

'Yes, I found some excellent plants in the forest.'

Even Dad was half smiling as he watched out of the window. 'Never send an army to fight on an empty stomach,' he said, getting into the ninjutsu philosophy himself now.

'The food will be delicious and they'll all eat loads,' Neena continued. 'And then they'll pay for it with very grumbly stomachs and extremely loose bowels. They'll be running to the toilet every two minutes and hopefully their fighting strength will be seriously diminished.'

'Good thinking, Neena,' I said. But I knew it would take an awful lot more than a few runny tummies to defeat the Kataki at midnight.

It was getting dark as I stood at the window, watching all the activity below. It was nearly the longest day, so I knew it was after ten o'clock already. Mad Dog was still sawing. Every so often he'd stop to get his breath. His hands were really sore now, where he'd been forcing the tiny blade back and forth with hardly anything to grip hold of. He beckoned me over and whispered to me, 'It's going to be one bar, that's all. Not sure if any of us'll be able to get through.'

'I can get through that,' I whispered back.

'I need to wait till we're ready now,' he said. 'Can't go taking the bar out and leaving a gap in case they see.'

Below us, the Kataki were checking their hang-gliding wings and packing them up to be carried to wherever they'd be launching themselves from. The empty shells of the bombs were being taken down to the dungeons and others were being brought back up. These were heavy, most likely filled with explosives, given the care everyone took handling them. The bombs were being stored in boxes, wrapped in straw, then loaded on a cart.

'How are we going to stop them, love?' Dad said. 'Have you got a plan?'

I smiled. I didn't have a plan, but from past experience I

completely trusted that, once I was out of our prison and at the reservoir, a plan would make itself clear to me. 'Still forming,' I said. Then I turned to Neena. 'Keep looking out for Bushi and Akira, won't you? They might still be alive.'

Mad Dog raised an eyebrow. 'Toby looked pretty convinced he had one of them in that bundle. It could still be that your mum managed to switch parcels without Toby knowing.'

'I know. But one of them might still be out there, if not both. You need to call for them from time to time.' I whistled softly to remind everyone how. Two notes the same for Bushi and one high, one low for Akira. I looked down, foolishly hoping my whistles would bring them running up the wall to greet me. They didn't.

'Okay, Mad Dog,' I said. 'Finish the job.'

'Hang on,' said Dad. 'Don't we need to get our plan sorted? Who goes out first, how are we going to get down, what do we do when we're at the bottom?'

Mad Dog gave the bar a mighty yank, twisted it and pulled again. It broke free. 'We don't,' he said. 'Don't even bother arguing, Ralph – this is Hattie's gig. Just Hattie – and she's going to be fine.'

I leant forward and pushed my head into the gap. It was so tight that, for a moment, I doubted even I could get through. But I was going to give it my best shot. I pulled back and turned to Dad.

'I can do this and I have no choice . . .' I calmly told him.

'No, no, no, Hattie,' he said. 'No way, not without me . . .'

'Mr Jackson,' Neena said politely and took his arm. He

shook her off. 'Hattie's our only chance, Mr Jackson,' she continued in her determined, Neena-like way. 'So please don't make this even harder for her.'

'Neena's right,' said Mad Dog, 'and besides, Hattie might be able to help us out from the other side.' He took off his watch and set the alarm as Neena spoke to Dad again.

'Mr Jackson – if Hattie doesn't go, just think what will happen to everyone who lives in the valley below the reservoir . . .'

'Raven's never going to find that dagger in the dam wall,' Dad said, exasperated.

'Exactly,' I smiled. 'So there's really no danger he's going to kill me with it – not yet anyway. But he is intending to blow up the dam wall and I have to stop him. It's my mission, remember?'

'Yes,' said Mad Dog. 'All those families you used to know in Falstone, Yarrow, Stannesburn . . . Hattie has to go out and try to protect them.' Mad Dog turned to me. 'I've set my watch for midnight, Hattie – your birthday. I have a feeling things might kick off with the scroll.' He put his watch on my wrist as Neena spoke.

'Not just the families, Mr Jackson, their children, their babies – but all their livestock, their homes, their heritage . . . Gone, for certain. Let Hattie go.' She took his arm again and this time he let her. He knew I had to do this; but I could tell every bone in his body was fighting to rush forward, grab me and impose a curfew and tell me he was the adult, that he was the policeman and he should be the one putting his life on the line for me.

I didn't even catch his eye. I turned back to the window and pushed my head hard into the gap between the end bar and the stone at the edge of the window. I held my ears tight against my head as I wiggled and dropped into the deepest Zen state I could manage. I needed that bar to be as kind to me as it possibly could – maybe it would even bend a little bit. Although it was set deep into the concrete, top and bottom, the bar suddenly rotated just a few millimetres. It was enough – the widest part of my head shot through and, by turning sideways, I could quickly follow with my shoulders, then my body, then my legs. I held on to the bars and squatted on the tiny ledge outside, looking round to see the best escape route. I pointed upwards to let the others know my plan, then put on my ninja hood, so I was dressed entirely in black and almost impossible to see against the dark stone work.

'Go, girl,' Mad Dog whispered, handing me the sawn-off bar. 'Be safe.' He held his hands out at the very top of the window, so I could use them as a step up. I tucked the bar into my belt and stepped on Mad Dog's hands. From there it was easy to clamber up the wall, using the rough stones to hold on to. I didn't look down, or back, or out to the perimeter walls to see if anyone was watching me. I moved as silently and as invisibly as I could, scaling the wall and hauling myself up on to the pitch roof that led from the top of the prison room to the wall of a smaller tower that topped this whole building. It was still raining and suddenly a bolt of lightning lit up the sky. I lay as flat as I could, not moving, hoping that no one had seen me.

The top of the smaller tower was another couple of metres above me but, before I climbed any higher, I set about doing the only thing I could think of to try and give the others a chance to escape. I loosened some tiles and pulled them free. They were made of slate, big and heavy, but I just managed to drag a couple sideways to make a hole in the roof.

I crawled across the tiles to the smaller tower and climbed up. I pulled myself cautiously on to the flat roof. It was a small area, inside the parapet walls – about three metres square. It was strange and rather spooky. The whole area was filled with straw, like a huge bird's nest. There were bones and skeletons of what looked like sheep and some half-eaten chickens and some discarded, rusty tools and weapons.

But best of all, lying there, like a gift from the universe, were Raven's old wings. As I scrambled across the roof, my foot caught on something buried in the straw. It was a rope. My heart leapt – especially when I found a couple more all twisted round each other, wet and dirty like they'd been there for months or even years. But that didn't matter, as long as they were still strong. I tied the longest one securely around the parapet, then attached the next one to it, and another, making sure there was at least ten metres. I tied some of the loose bones to the end so the weight would pull the rope in the direction I needed it to go, then I let the bones slip down the pitch roof towards the hole I'd made when I removed the slates. The bones disappeared into the hole, into the prison room. They carried on down, down, then stopped. I felt a tug and knew that meant it had reached the others. Hopefully they'd be able to make it out now as well. Mad Dog was great at climbing ropes and, even if Dad and Neena couldn't, Mad Dog would come up here and find a way to help them with all these discarded tools and weapons. I didn't have time to do any more for them. I filled my pockets with every tool I could fit in – climbing claws, flints, some old rag covered in mud. I didn't care – I just wanted anything that might be useful. I bundled some rope into my pocket, then I used a short piece of twine to tie the prison-cell bar on to my back.

I stood on the edge of the parapet to decide which direction to go. Hardly anyone was around. I could see the cart loaded with bombs far off in the distance, with a trail of Kataki walking behind it, each carrying their rolled up wings and harnesses. They were heading up towards the forest, so I still couldn't tell where they were going to launch from. Only a couple of sentries had been left to guard the castle compound and they were on the far wall, crossing over as they patrolled in opposite directions. This was my chance – I had to set off now, gliding out over the perimeter, while they were both as far as they'd ever be from me. I hauled the wings on to my back and secured them really tightly. They were twice the size of the ones I'd arrived in and I felt a little insecure – especially as I could tell straight away that one wing was heavier than the other, no doubt because of Raven's lopsided body. His wings had been counterbalanced to keep him stable. I'd have to compensate to keep my balance. Breathing deeply to keep calm, I picked up a brick in my right hand to match the weighted left wing, then I launched myself from the top of the tower into the darkness.

CHAPTER TWELVE

'The present is a ninja's only opportunity for power.'

I swooped over the castle walls, nervous this time about whether my wings would carry me. I needn't have worried. They were perfectly crafted to do this. Although they were much bigger, they were a lot lighter than the ones I'd flown in on and designed to support someone much heavier than me. The wind had dropped considerably and the rain had stopped, but a tiny gust was still enough to lift me up and carry me high into the sky. Another great advantage was that Raven's superior wings moved as though hinged, so they could be outstretched to glide or swept back to make me more aerodynamic, like a bird of prey when it swoops and dives towards its prey.

As I floated above the forest, back up the valley towards Kielder reservoir, I wondered for the first time what the real reason was that our *jonin* hadn't just gone to the police. How could we all be in this position, facing the dam being blown up, risking the lives of hundreds of people in the valley below? For a second, I thought, *Shouldn't I be heading down the valley and telling all those people to get out, to leave their homes because if they stay they might drown?* But that wasn't my mission. My mission was to stop the dam being blown up – and it was nearly midnight anyway. It would probably takes ages to persuade people I wasn't some crazy girl, knocking on their door with an unlikely story about ninja villains with a brutal leader who had such a strong animus he seemed to believe he was half-raven. Even then, wouldn't they just go to check the dam? If Raven's plan was successful, they'd all be drowned as they made their way up the valley. At this late stage, I knew I'd never persuade Raven the dagger wasn't buried there. No, the only thing to do now was to get to the dam wall and try and stop the attack altogether.

I could see the massive expanse of reservoir water glistening in the moonlight. The wind dropped as though the bad weather had just blown through. This wasn't good news for me because, even though I don't weigh much, I needed some gusts to help me hang-glide nearer the reservoir. I was starting to lose altitude, so I tried out these super special wings and pushed them back, stretching my body like an arrow and aiming myself towards the reservoir, trying to cover as much distance as I could. I flew down, down, down, eventually landing silently on top of a clump of trees. I was glad of all the training I'd done with Yazuki. I balanced perfectly, even with the huge wings, and managed to undo the harness and wriggle my way out, pushing the wings into the dense foliage so they wouldn't be seen by anyone flying over.

My heart was beating quite fast now. I knew there wasn't much time. I sped off through the trees, jumping from branch to branch, climbing down then back up whenever I needed to. If I could have taken it slowly, I would have made my way to the forest floor and crept silently from tree to tree, but the Kataki army were supposedly making their strike at midnight and I was rapidly running out of time.

Eventually, I came to the edge of the forest, below the high bank that led up to the top of the dam wall. I could just make out the valve tower, rising out of the water. Something moved. I ducked down as a looming figure appeared on top of the tower, raising its giant wings. It was Raven. He turned on a light and shone it down on to the water for a very short time. It flashed off and on a couple of times, marking where the Kataki should drop their bombs.

I crawled up the bank for a better view, and could now make out several figures posted around the edge of the reservoir. There was no way I could take on all these people – and I had no idea how many more might be hiding in the woods. I had to assume other people were also in the area, maybe some people on our side as well – hopefully, Mum and Yazuki. And with any luck, Mad Dog and Neena might find their way here with Dad and, although they wouldn't have any specific instructions, I'd certainly feel a lot happier knowing they were here, trying their best to help me. But for the moment it was just me, on my own. It would be better for everyone if these Kataki sentries were somehow disabled. I thought back, remembering what Yazuki had taught me: *'Guards are most vulnerable when attacked from the water. That's the last place they'll be expecting you.'*

I took the rope from my pocket and used the sharp flint to cut it into lengths of about a metre. I pulled out the muddy rag I'd picked up from Raven's nest on the top of the tower and tore it into strips. I gathered up leaves that I could roll into a big ball to stuff in each guard's mouth before I gagged them so they couldn't shout. I stored all these things in different pockets so I could lay my hands on them in an instant. Next, I had to somehow get into the reservoir without anyone spotting me.

That was easier than I'd expected. I scrambled back down the bank and ran across the bottom of the dam wall until I got to the bank on the other side. I climbed up and was immediately at the edge of the visitors' centre. It was deserted, just as I'd expected – but there were CCTV cameras covering the whole area. I wondered if I should just start screaming and waving until a night watchman or the police came and I could beg them to patrol the dam and not let the Kataki blow it up. But I didn't know who was already on the Kataki's side. Takumi had been very clear there were infiltrators in high places. And what if they didn't believe me? Besides, it was no good just delaying Raven, I needed to put an end to his plans once and for all.

I didn't step into the car park. Instead I kept to the shadows behind the back of the visitors' centre, then wriggled on my stomach down to the water's edge. I could see my first guard about fifty metres away. He was more isolated than the others, probably because this area was better lit by the car park lights and Raven would be able to see any intruders from his vantage point on top of the valve tower. Swimming fifty metres underwater was nothing for me. I took a few very deep breaths and closed my eyes. I felt my blood getting rich with oxygen, almost to the point where I felt light-headed. Then I slipped into the reservoir and opened my eyes. By keeping out any light until this moment, I could see really well through the murky water. I swam slow, careful strokes, checking the structure of the dam, relieved there were concrete posts set in the water every so often. I needed these to carry out my plan. I looked up, searching for the shape of the guard standing on the bank above me, silhouetted in the moonlight.

I broke the surface of the water without a sound, just my face emerging so I could check he wasn't looking. He was still facing in the opposite direction. I pulled myself on to the bank in one silent movement, taking out my makeshift gag and a ball of leaves. I reached over the guard's head, pausing just long enough for him to realise he was being attacked from behind. As he opened his mouth to shout, I jammed the leaves into his mouth and tied the gag so fast he didn't know what had happened. He swung round, exactly as I hoped he would and I caught his arm and twisted it hard, forcing him on to his knees on the ground. I fell on top of him and tied his feet in seconds, knowing that legs can do much more damage than arms. I tied his hands as he looked at me, wide-eyed in terror, his nostrils flaring as he panicked, using all his energy just to keep breathing. He was a novice, that was clear. And from the sound of his gurgling stomach, Neena's laxative supper had started working and had already significantly weakened him. But any ninja worth their salt would keep calm at this point, knowing there would be a thousand ways to fight me if they just kept their wits about them. But this guard was panicking and it was clear that Raven really had formed his army quickly and had not paid proper attention to training the newcomers.

I didn't want to seriously hurt anyone, but I had to make sure the guard couldn't escape or raise the alarm. There were some reeds growing at the edge of the lake, so I plucked one and made sure it was big enough to breathe through. I pushed the guard into the reservoir, getting in beside him and pulled him down. Before his head sank under the water, I whispered, 'In through your mouth, out through your nose – don't bite on the reed and keep moving to stay warm.' When his head was ten centimetres below the surface, I tied him to one of the posts so he couldn't move. I undid the gag, pulled out the bundle of leaves and put the reed into his mouth instead. He inhaled a huge gulp of air and then bubbles came out through his nose. I knew he could stay like that for a while if he had to. I gave him the thumbs up and swam off.

I grabbed an armful of reeds, swimming a short distance before surfacing and hiding amongst some boats that were moored to a wooden jetty. I could see five other Kataki around the perimeter of the water. With the reeds, and the rope and the strips of old rag, I'd be able to disable them all quite quickly; but I couldn't risk Raven getting suspicious if he realised his sentries were disappearing. I decided to deal with the three furthest from him, then take out the remaining two at the very last minute.

I still had no idea how I was going to stop the air strike. It was obviously important that Raven shone his lamp to tell the hang-gliders the exact point where the bombs had to be dropped. Then they would bounce along the surface of the water, hitting the dam wall at exactly the right spot before detonating at their pre-set depth and blasting a massive hole. Maybe I could get to the top of the valve tower and disable the light somehow. That might be enough to cause the mission to fail.

I shut my eyes, breathed deeply then went through the same process with guard number two, swimming underwater, rising silently up and out of the reservoir to grab him from behind, gag him, tie his feet and his hands, then rolling him silently into the water and tying him to a post with just a solitary reed to breathe through. Number two seemed even younger and less experienced than number one – and was also much weaker than he should have been.

However, number three was older and heavier and put up much more of a fight. He nearly landed on me as I twisted his arm. I rolled out of the way but didn't make much impact sitting on him to tie his feet. I managed to carry out exactly the same plan but guessed I'd have a nasty bruise where he clobbered me with his elbow as I fought to tie his hands.

Just three more to go. But as I swam silently towards guard number four, something completely unexpected happened. By chance, Raven swung his light across the lake and caught me like a startled rabbit. I dipped back under the water, but I was sure anyone looking would have seen me. And they had. As I resurfaced, I could just make out a figure, lowering themselves into the water and swimming towards me. Fighting underwater was not something I wanted to get involved with, so I pulled myself up and scrambled on to the bank. But when I looked round, I saw the figure had already turned back and was clinging for dear life at the edge of the reservoir.

'Mad Dog?' I whispered, relieved but scared. What was he doing in the water?!

He crawled round the bank towards me. 'Your dad worked it out!' he whispered. 'He got it – *Tanil, Latin, wage war!*'

In the distance I heard a twig snap and then another. Through the darkness my sharp eyes could make out four Kataki coming towards us – more than I thought were left on guard. Then two more appeared from the trees. I'd seriously underestimated how many people Raven had brought to protect him while the rest of his army made their way to the hang-gliding launch point. Although Raven had turned off the light, the moon was bright enough for me to see that we were only seconds away from being surrounded.

'To *wage war* is *belligerare* in Latin,' Mad Dog continued.

'Your dad remembered another quote Jacko used to show him at the Imperial War Museum! The root word – *Bell*.'

'*Bell* . . . ? The bell tower?'

'He's gone there to look for the dagger.'

'The sunken village?' My heart lurched, terrified at the idea of Dad setting off, unprepared, to dive down into the murky darkness of Kielder reservoir. I wanted to scream and panic – I had no idea what to do. I didn't mind putting myself at risk, but I couldn't bear the idea of something happening to Dad. With all these Kataki moving in on us, I didn't even know how I could go and help him. But then the next surprise came flying from the forest to greet me.

A monkey shadow leapt, screeching, at one of the approaching guards. Then the monkey shadow turned into a cat shadow who turned into me! I swear it's true: the monkey shadow whipped off its hood and there I was! It was just like looking in the mirror. The Kataki all looked round, gasping as they saw me miraculously appearing on their side of the reservoir. Mad Dog took the chance to run at the nearest Kataki and push him to the ground, while I slid silently into the water and submerged my body without making a ripple. And then the real fighting began!

As I swam away underwater I could see their silhouettes on the bank. After about twenty metres I put my head up to take a breath. I watched just for a moment in absolute amazement – the 'me' who'd arrived to help Mad Dog was carrying out some of the best leg kicks and unarmed combat I'd ever done! Even I felt taken in, watching this person with my face, my hair. It felt like a lifetime since I'd last seen Yazuki, but I was pretty convinced from the monkey movements that this was her now, impersonating me and carrying out one of the greatest ninjutsu deceits – *making many appear as one*. It was the perfect use of the masks she'd insisted on making in my bedroom, only a few days before.

In front of my eyes, the Yazuki version of me kicked and somersaulted and disabled two Kataki with the most amazing skill. By slamming her foot into one of their necks, Yazuki caught the paralysis spot and made Hattori Hachi's enemy fall motionless to the ground. I have to say, my skill was very impressive.

But no sooner had I arrived, than I disappeared. Then I reappeared – on the other side of the lake this time! There was a ferocious roar and Raven's light came on just long enough to reveal a panther shape on top of the valve tower next to him. The panther jumped from the tower into the water and swam to where the new me had appeared. That 'me' held up an arm to reveal a massive Samurai sword. Toby pounced from the water – and held up an equally terrifying sword. The fighting started and I could see sparks from fifty metres away. Again, the new me wasn't wearing a ninja hood and it was clear to anyone it was Hattori Hachi, sword fighting Toby with incredible skill. The Kataki nearest Mad Dog gasped and I heard him say, 'It *is* her!' She can appear and disappear at will!'

I was relieved the Kataki hadn't had much training and were all falling for this very ancient ninja trick. It *was* pretty incredible, watching multiple versions of me, convincing the Kataki that I was somehow superhuman. And I have to say, if this was Mum being me now – which I was pretty sure it was – she was clearly one of the best sword fighters in the world. I still had no idea if Toby was pretending to fight her, or whether she was really trying to kill him but, whichever way, I had to leave them to it. Something else was happening that needed my attention . . .

It started very softly but it was a sound I'd grown to know quite well. The strange, haunting, watery sound of the sunken village church's tolling bell, always when the reservoir was low and the wind was in the right direction. But right now, the reservoir was high and the air was completely still. There was not a whisper of breeze, so it definitely wasn't the wind causing it to make that chilling sound. It must be Dad, needing help!

I knew from what Dad had told me that the village was right by the jetty where people water-skied. I could see the jetty in the distance, about three hundred metres from me. I let out all my breath so I would sink back under the water and took my first stroke, using the moon to guide me as I moved in the direction of the sunken village. For a second I was torn – my instructions had been very clear. *Find out exactly what Raven is planning and stop him.* I was supposed to stop Raven blowing up the dam wall but the bell was sounding again now, louder. It was as though it was drawing me towards it, the strikes closer together, more insistent. How could I ignore Dad if he was in trouble?

But then it hit me – Raven was looking for the

190

Diamond Dagger, so if I could find it and show it to him, then he'd have no reason to blow up the dam. So I was doing the right thing after all!

I swam on, faster now, less worried about making ripples as I was further from the Kataki and knew Mum and Yazuki were keeping them all busy. I couldn't afford to get too out of breath as I'd need to be calm when I got to the sunken village. I rolled on to my back underwater then surfaced, pushing up my face so I could breathe until I felt my blood rich with oxygen again. I could feel the tolling bell reverberating through my body. I knew I was close. Still I kept my eyes shut, knowing I would need the best night vision underwater. I dipped back down, pulling myself deep into the reservoir, away from the surface, nearer and nearer the tolling bell. Then I opened my eyes.

The eeriest thing greeted me. There was the outline of a whole deserted village. Houses, still with roofs intact, dry stone walls, even a little bridge on the bottom of the lake, now going nowhere. I could only see the buildings nearest me at first, but as I slowed down and squinted I could make out what looked like a small school and then, at the furthest point, a tower, rising above the other buildings.

The church.

Something moved – hardly any distance away. It was a dark figure, just like me, dressed in black, head covered in a ninja hood, wriggling and slithering like some scary sea serpent. Someone else was down here besides Dad. I swam down to where the old school building would shield me from view. Time was running out and, even though the bell had stopped ringing, I knew I had to get inside that bell tower fast.

With renewed energy, I swam towards the tower. I could have gone inside the church and found the steps that led up to the top, but I took a risk. I guessed there would be openings at the top of the tower to allow the sound of the bell to travel. This would be a much easier way in for me – I just had to hope the gaps were big enough for me to squeeze through. The top of the tower was about three metres below the surface of the lake. I wasn't remotely out of breath – I think a lot of adrenalin had kicked in but I knew this could be a lengthy struggle, so I made my way behind the tower, swam up to the surface, eyes closed once again, and took another eight deep breaths.

As I headed back down towards the tower, I opened my eyes. There were large gaps in each wall just below the pitch roof of the bell tower, easily wide enough for me to squeeze through. I pulled myself inside the tower and pressed against the outside of the bell. It was really dark – almost totally black. I started to feel my way around. The bell itself was as smooth as anything. There was no dagger hidden on the outside. I felt up to the top to see how the bell was attached to the roof. There was a wooden cross-beam, which was already very rotten, no doubt because of the years it had been underwater. The chain that held the bell in place felt completely normal, though I could feel soft algae growing over it. The bell itself was about a metre and a half high, so I felt my way down the outside, very careful not to disturb it, then swam up inside the bell.

The first thing I felt was the large ball of metal that was the ringer. Of course the dagger could be anywhere, in this whole bell tower – but I felt sure the Kataki would have checked it thoroughly over the years. Great-granddad Jacko must have done something really smart. The water surged up towards me and I knew that meant someone was moving around below. I let go of all anxiety and focused on what I was there to do. I'd already used about half my air, so I had to be quick.

I felt inside the bell, running my hand in a spiral, working my way down. It was smooth. So then I pulled myself up and sat myself on the ringer, wrapping myself around it so that, if it moved, my body would hit the metal first and hopefully not make a sound. I couldn't afford to draw attention to what I was doing. I felt along the metal bar that attached the ringer to the inside of the bell. It was a square-shaped rod and as I ran my hand up it, *Ouch!* Something sharp jabbed my hand. I reached further up – there was definitely something there! Old leather straps were holding something in place – one at the bottom and, as I felt higher, I found another right up where the rod was fixed to the inside of the top of the bell itself. My fingers were icy cold and not working too well, but even so, I pulled at the end of the first strap and undid the buckle, which must have been really rusty. I could feel now this was definitely a long blade. Further up, there was a handle at the top – which felt exactly like a dagger! What else could it possibly be, hidden inside the bell? Smart Great-granddad Jacko must have concealed the dagger here before the Kataki found him. Dad had said most of his family were bell ringers – why hadn't I thought of this before?

I grabbed the second strap and wrenched it undone. I was just about to pull the dagger out of its hiding place when the bell suddenly shifted and slipped, as though the cross-beam that was holding us up was breaking because of my extra weight. The ringer thumped against my body and forced some very precious air out of my lungs, trapping me against the inside of the bell.

Below, I could just make out two figures, fighting, as they appeared up some spiral stairs and on to the platform below the bell. They were pushing and pulling at each other's necks. A foot came flying upwards as the one in a full ninja outfit forced the other one's arm behind his back. No shoes – just a sock with a hole in the toe, which I recognised immediately. It was Dad! And he was fighting like a demon – using every bit of his police training and diving experience. But I could see he was no real match for his Kataki opponent.

I doubled my efforts, wriggling and pushing the ringer and suddenly I was free. I shifted just enough to drop away from the bell, pulling the dagger behind me. As it sliced against the ringer, there was a metallic sound that travelled through the water, making my hair stand on end. It was sharp and ear-splitting and rang out louder and longer than I'd have expected. The fighters stopped grappling for a second and looked up. I pushed myself down towards them, swimming through a shaft of moonlight that illuminated the dagger. Even though I was underwater and rapidly running out of breath, I nearly gasped. The dagger's handle was encrusted with diamonds the size of peas, just as Ridley had said. It was the most beautiful thing I'd ever laid eyes on. All the algae that had gathered over the years was just falling away, as though the Diamond Dagger had special powers! In between the diamonds there were all kinds of symbols and Japanese characters engraved. It felt as though the diamonds were shining so brightly, they were illuminating the bell tower! I could see Dad's face clearly now, his face red as though he was out of air and about to inhale a lungful of water.

Things were easier with this dagger in my hands. For a start, the blade was half a metre long – and as sharp as anything. It wasn't like any normal dagger: the way it looked and the noise it made let me know it was crafted from the finest metal. It was light but strong, with a gleaming tip that ended in the sharpest point imaginable. It felt as though it had a life of its own, seeming to pull me down to the Kataki, who still had Dad in a stranglehold. Of course I know a dagger can't have a life of its own – it was probably because I'd been told it was legendary that my body was giving it life in my hands. But whatever was driving me, the Kataki took one look at the dagger, let go of Dad and backed off as fast as he could.

I didn't go after him – Dad really needed my help. I reached down and grabbed his arm, and not before time. As I pulled him up beside the bell, the cross-beam gave way and the bell fell to the platform, making a terrible, vibrating, tolling sound. We had to get out fast – the ringing was bound to bring more Kataki looking for us. I swam through the gap at the top of the tower and pulled Dad after me. Although he was nearly out of air, he wasn't panicking. He swam past me to the surface, pushed his face up and just lay there, gulping huge breaths. I came up beside him – and immediately saw that there was going to be no pausing for either of us.

High above, far in the distance, twenty Kataki warriors were hang-gliding toward Kielder reservoir, each carrying a deadly bomb intended to cause untold death and devastation to the surrounding area.

CHAPTER THIRTEEN

'Fight your enemy's weakest points.'

At least I was now in possession of the Diamond Dagger. If I could just show it to Raven, surely I could stop the attack on the dam. I wasn't going to let anyone touch it – not even Dad. But as we got out of the water, he had other ideas.

'Hattie! They'll kill you with it! Throw it back in the water! You have to get rid of it!'

I knew that was just Dad panicking, so I ran for cover in the trees. Dad followed but I was faster than him. I just kept running back along the length of the reservoir. Even though I had to keep focused on the task ahead, I kept looking down at this dagger. I couldn't help myself. It was just so stunning. As I glanced back, I saw Dad was transfixed as well, his eyes glued to it as he ran after me.

'Split up,' I said, running ahead. I needed a clear mind and in this state Dad would confuse me and also be an easy target for the enemy. 'Keep hidden and out of the way. Don't do anything – especially near Toby. Let the people who know what they're doing sort this out, Dad.' I was already tying the dagger on to my back with the last of the rope. I jumped up and pulled myself into a tree.

'No, Hattie —' Dad protested, but I was already flying off through the foliage, swinging and climbing where I knew he couldn't follow. The hang-gliders had launched from Berrymoor Edge up near the military range, which was good news as it might give me a few extra precious minutes. I glanced at Mad Dog's watch – seven minutes to midnight. Seven minutes was about the time it would take the flying Kataki to arrive.

It didn't take long for me to be back where I'd started, right alongside the valve tower. I looked around. Everyone had disappeared. No fighting, and no guards on the lake perimeter either. But Raven was still up on the tower, flashing the lamp as he lined it up to the exact point the Kataki had to drop their bombs.

Swoosh! I drew the dagger from where I'd tied it and felt my whole body come alive. The sound it made was almost magical and it gleamed as I brandished it, attracting light and reflecting it back, beautiful and mysterious. The diamonds glistened even in this gentle moonlight. I jumped down out of the tree and ran to the edge of the reservoir.

'Is this what you're looking for?' I shouted up to Raven. If there was no reason to blow up the dam, surely he'd turn that light off and the Kataki wouldn't drop their bombs?

I heard a groan. For a second it confused me. It wasn't

coming from Raven and I couldn't see anyone else, apart from the hang-gliders closing in on us. It sounded again – a low moan. I looked around.

There was a deep laugh from the other direction as, above, Raven sneered at me with a horrible sarcastic noise, like a bird cackling or cawing malevolently.

'So you claim to bring me the very weapon I will slay you with,' he boomed in his rasping, Japanese accent. 'How very kind and thoughtful. But I doubt even you would be so stupid. I have no need of your fake dagger!'

He turned on the lamp.

'No!' I shouted. 'There's no need to blow up the dam. This is the Diamond Dagger, come and look!'

'If you want to stop me, show me the scroll,' he said. 'If you have the scroll and the dagger I can kill you with, then I might be interested!'

I was completely at a loss. I'd felt sure the dagger would be enough to bring him down from the valve tower. And I didn't know who had the scroll. If Toby had disappeared, did that mean he had it? That perhaps he was no longer working with Raven? I had to think faster than ever. Across the reservoir I could see Kataki rescuing the guards I'd tied up underwater. They'd soon be back to fight and meanwhile, twenty airborne Kataki with bombs were but moments away . . .

Okay, if Raven wasn't going to come to me, then I'd have to go up to him. As I took the first step towards the water, I heard the low moan again. This time a weak voice murmured, 'Hachi!'

I peered into the undergrowth – and was horrified to see Mum, blood on her face, holding an empty cardboard tube. She called louder this time, 'Toby attacked me! He's taken the scroll!' In fact, she called so loud, I was sure Raven must have heard. I crouched down, wondering why Mum was being so careless but she whispered, 'No! Hattie – leave me, I'm okay!' I could see immediately the blood was fake but I had no idea what Mum was up to.

I ran full tilt to the edge of the reservoir and was about to jump into the water to swim to the valve tower when there was a roar – and Toby appeared! He came bounding up the grassy bank, holding the scroll in his hand.

'It's me!' he shouted up to Raven. 'I have it and I'm going to sign it and then I will have control of the whole Hattori estate and all the wealth and power of the Golden Child will belong to us, the Kataki, and to you our noble leader! Two minutes until midnight, then I will sign and it will all be ours!'

I didn't know what Toby was up to, but I had the Diamond Dagger in my possession that could kill him if he signed the ancient document and became the Golden Child. So actually, I still had the upper hand. The dagger made me feel unbelievably powerful and strong. I could kill whoever I wanted, take whatever I thought was mine, harm and maim anyone and end up in Raven's position up there on top of the tower, controlling his evil band of followers. I felt possessed as I ran at Toby, making a strange guttural noise that didn't sound like me at all. I swiped at him, so near to his face, I nearly cut off his nose.

'Hattie!' he yelled. But I wasn't listening. I swiped again and this time he fled. I ran after him as he tried to get away into the trees, but I was faster and more agile than I'd ever been. As he climbed a tree, I ran up the next one, jumping across so I was above him. But in my fearless state, I hadn't thought things through. Toby reached out and pulled a Samurai sword from where it was concealed in the foliage. Of course! He'd pre-set all his tools and weapons like any good ninja would!

Schoooom! He stopped my next strike dead, dropping the scroll into one of his deep pockets.

'Hattie, stop!' I heard Mum call out. But the dagger had somehow taken over my mind. It was fighting Toby steel on steel, making dents in his sword, my dagger was so powerful. I wasn't in control at all. But neither was I alone. Mad Dog suddenly appeared right above me with a long piece of wood. Together, we chased Toby back down the tree, and while Mad Dog fought him plank to sword as best he could, I used the Diamond Dagger to slit open Toby's pocket so the scroll fell out. I somersaulted underneath his feet to catch it, just hearing Mum shout again, 'HATTIE! STOP!' But I just wasn't listening. I grabbed the scroll and fled.

Above me, Raven was flexing his wings, watching as Toby and Mad Dog fought. He'd left the light shining on the water as twenty Kataki started swooping down over the reservoir, preparing to drop their bombs. A loud bleeping sound caught me unaware – coming from my wrist! Mad Dog's watch, set for the moment of my sixteenth birthday.

It was going off! It was midnight!

I reached in my secret trouser pocket for the pen Takumi had given me and held up the scroll. I had to stop the Kataki from dropping their bombs!

'It's here!' I shouted up at Raven. 'The scroll – look!'

'Hattie, NO!' Mum shrieked, running towards me, not injured at all. Toby was at her side. Although I could hear Mum shouting, the dagger seemed to be willing me on. Then a voice deep inside my head made me do it. I just *felt* this command: *Sign, Hattori Hachi, it is your destiny.*

So I signed the scroll, in front of all of them.

As I wrote my name in indelible ink at the bottom of the list of all the previous Golden Children, I heard Mum's voice ring out, 'Hattie, don't sign – he'll kill you!'

Too late. As Mum ran towards me, I looked down at my best handwriting and wondered what kind of future I'd just brought upon myself.

'Oh Hattie, Hattie,' she whispered, blind terror in her eyes. 'You weren't supposed to get the scroll!'

'What's going on, Mum?' But there was no time for her to reply. There was just a horrible shriek from above our heads as Raven's light went off and he launched himself from the top of the valve tower.

'You have failed me Toby!' he screamed. 'You are not the Golden Child!'

'Run and don't look back,' Mum whispered.

I just had time to ask, 'Is Toby one of us?' before a huge black shadow blocked out the moon as Raven swooped down, spreading his enormous wings.

'Yes,' she whispered back.

'I must see that scroll!' came Raven's screeching voice as Toby ran towards him, acting brilliantly.

'It's real, I've seen it, I'll take care of her!' he shouted.

'THEN SHE MUST DIE!' came Raven's order. 'KILL HER – OR I WILL!'

With Raven's light switched off and no visual clue to guide them, the bomb-bearing Kataki flew right over our heads, heading back down the valley towards the castle. One last straggler slowed down, then turned and circled overhead. Almost in slow motion, the hang-glider undid the leather straps.

One lone bomb fell from its casing.

Down, down, down, towards us.

BOOM! It exploded right beside me in the water, momentarily distracting Raven and Toby. The force blew me backwards as, above me, Raven screeched with fury and swooped towards the lone Kataki in a full-scale attack.

It was as though the centre of the earth had erupted as the ground shook and a deep, low rumble echoed all around. Where the bomb had dropped, the water started to move in slow motion – first dipping in level, then forced back up by the energy that the explosive had released deep in the reservoir. A column rose up like some great fountain or a tsunami. Concrete flew everywhere as the sluice gate to the overflow tunnel was blown to pieces. Water started flooding out of the reservoir, down the overflow pipe, towards the castle.

The lone Kataki discarded their wings mid-air and dropped into a tree, leaving Raven soaring high above.

There was a triumphant screech and the escaping figure scampered off like a monkey. It had to be Yazuki!

Raven swooped towards me, his talons swiping angrily as he tried to grab the scroll. There was no way I was letting him take it from me. I held it tightly under my arm as I ducked, rolled, grabbed a rock and threw it hard at Raven, springing to my feet again. The tremors from the explosion brought at least another ten Kataki running from the undergrowth, coming to see what was happening. I wanted to flee but suddenly Dad was there, wearing a Hattori Hachi face mask, eyes on fire as he saw Raven circling above me. It was as though our whole family was psychically linked – along with Yazuki, Neena and Takumi, who I recognised from his tiny gnarled hands as he ran from the forest. All of them were coming to protect me, all now looking like me, including Mum! I could tell from their bodies who was who. Yazuki must have made quite a few of those Hattori masks! We all burst into action, picking up sticks or using daggers or throwing stars or Samurai swords – whatever each of us had to hand.

But none of it tricked Raven – he knew I was the one who'd signed the scroll. He swooped again, his evil metal talons gleaming.

That's when he saw the Diamond Dagger up close. I heard him gasp.

'It's genuine!' he exclaimed. 'Then I will kill you with it!' Raven was possessed. His eyes bored into mine and for a moment it was as though he was brainwashing me. My mind linked with his and I felt the worst terror I'd experienced in my life. I was consumed with hatred, loathing and the desire to kill. I was being sucked right inside Raven's mind and, for an instant, I understood what it was like to feel the way he did. I fought to banish these thoughts. My feet were rooted to the spot as I came back to my senses, looking up at him. Then he hit me so hard, the dagger flew from my hand, spiralling up into the air. Raven grabbed it and swooped skywards again. But I wasn't going to let a deranged man with a dagger end my life this way – not without putting up my best fight ever.

As he flew back down, taking back his arm, aiming to strike at my neck and cut off my head, I dropped into my Zen-like state and my body went into slow motion. From standing, I suddenly inverted my whole body, kicking both legs high above my head. I cartwheeled in the air without even putting my hands down. I scored a direct hit right under Raven's chin, knocking his head back and winding him. I landed upright on the ground. I don't know how he managed to recover so quickly, but he swooped back up into the air.

'That will be your last ever kick, you pitiful child!' he screamed. But I knew that if he wanted to kill me with that dagger, he'd have to get close again – and now Mum and Yazuki, Dad, Neena and Takumi were all surrounding me, forming an impenetrable circle of protection. Only Mad Dog was missing.

Mum whispered, 'Don't fight Raven, Hattie, he'll kill you. Stay with us, let Toby get the dagger, he'll find a way out of this . . .'

But I didn't want protecting – I was sick of Raven and his mindless brutality. I wanted to take him on and end this horrendous bullying, and get my hands back on that Diamond Dagger. It was as though some of its power had rubbed off on me and deep down, for the first time in my life, I felt ready to kill for it.

I ducked down and rolled past everyone's feet, shouting for Raven to come after me. Yazuki yelled, 'Don't do it Hattie, he'll kill you!'

'Nooooo!' I shouted back. I grabbed Mum's Samurai sword and ran at Raven, who dropped down to within five metres of the ground, brandishing the Diamond Dagger. It was almost glowing. I knew for sure it had powers beyond its use as a weapon. And I knew I would fail if I gave in to my desire to look at it.

I used all my energy and focused on Raven. What were his weaknesses? How could I defeat him? The answer came to me. The wings I'd used to escape the tower had been weighted off-centre. Raven had trouble balancing, because his left side was burnt and his ear had been destroyed in the fire at the hospital all those years ago. If I could bring him down to the ground, he'd be at a real disadvantage. It wasn't the dagger I needed to focus on, it was Raven's wings.

As he came towards me, the dagger pointing at my face, I crouched, then jumped into the nearest tree, pulling myself on to an overhanging branch. I was up on my feet in a second, balancing perfectly. I ran to the end of the branch where I now fought Raven face to face, sword on dagger, metal sparking, blades gleaming in the moonlight, with just the sound of slicing and blocking and our breaths as we fought like demons.

I sliced right through Raven's left wing. Raven tilted, off-balance, but righted himself immediately and started flying away from me. I took a big risk and jumped on to his back, even though we were five metres from the ground.

The second our bodies touched I was consumed with the memories of the fire when Raven was so badly burnt. Everywhere, people were yelling and screaming as thick smoke and searing flames engulfed us. But this time, I didn't let the horror overwhelm me. I gripped even tighter. With my weight added to his, we rolled and plummeted. I attacked his back with my Samurai sword, making sure both wings were completely destroyed. We sped towards the ground like two great big sacks of potatoes.

At the very last moment, I shut my eyes and relaxed. I felt Raven hit the ground before I felt the impact on my own body. He gasped and cried out at the same time as twenty Kataki and all my friends and family rushed in. The air was forced from my lungs and for a moment I felt light-headed. But Raven had broken my fall, and that gave me an advantage – though he was the one with the Diamond Dagger, and that would be making him feel invincible. I did a move I'd practised many times – the same move that only days ago Mad Dog had inflicted on me. I reached up under Raven's arms, forcing his shoulders back in *ryoyokudori*, or 'catching both wings'. This time there were real wings to deal with as I felt my way through piles of torn fabric to grab his fingers on both hands, bending and twisting each one, causing him excruciating pain. Of course it meant I couldn't take the dagger, but I didn't care – because Raven couldn't hold on to it now either. It fell to the ground, tantalisingly close, but I refused to look at it, even now. I knew the temptation would be to go for it expecting it could save my life – but the safest thing right now was to disable Raven. I didn't think any of his warriors would dare to use the Diamond Dagger on me – I was sure Raven wanted the prize of killing me to be his. I twisted and bent his fingers as he wailed like a baby and I thought to myself how pathetic bullies always are when someone finally hurts them.

Toby was the first to reach us, roaring and his eyes shining red – I didn't even see where he came from. He snatched up the Diamond Dagger and lifted it high in the air. I held Raven tight, just hoping Toby really was on our side and would kill Raven, not me. The fact that neither Mum nor Yazuki was rushing in to stop him gave me great hope that this terrible ordeal would soon be over. As I held my eyes tight shut, waiting for the impact of the dagger as it was thrust into Raven's heart, all I could hear was the water, still gushing from the reservoir into the overspill pipe, with the sound of sirens in the distance. Fire engines and police cars were on their way, so whatever Toby was going to do, he'd have to be quick. Then I heard a helicopter approaching overhead.

I waited for what seemed an age – but no strike came. I opened my eyes and involuntarily shouted, 'No!'

Mad Dog was creeping up on Toby, unseen and unheard. Suddenly, he grabbed him from behind, tearing the Diamond Dagger from his hand and forcing it against his neck. He had no idea Toby was intending to kill Raven, not me.

'What kind of father are you!' Mad Dog screamed at Dad. 'Letting this monster kill your daughter. He's evil, he's a traitor!' He pulled the dagger even closer to Toby's neck. I could see from the look on Dad's face that he now knew Toby was on our side and that somehow we had to stop Mad Dog – but we couldn't shout to tell Mad Dog not to hurt Toby. At that moment, it looked as though Toby was about to kill me and we couldn't risk the Kataki thinking we knew otherwise, or the whole of Raven's army would be down on us in seconds and we'd all be dead! We were at stalemate – me holding Raven and Mad Dog holding Toby.

It was Mr Bell we all missed. As I gripped tightly on to Raven's arms, bending his fingers so he couldn't move, a rat shadow suddenly ran at Mad Dog. What could I do? Someone had to stop Mad Dog from hurting Toby, so I had no choice but to let Mr Bell attack.

'MAD DOG! BEHIND!' Neena yelled, but too late.

Mr Bell thwacked Mad Dog with a plank, just like he had all that time ago in Camden. Back then, Mad Dog fell into the canal, only a couple of metres deep. But this was different. What happened next surely had to be the end of him. The force of the strike was so hard, Mad Dog flew sideways into the reservoir, right where water was still gushing down the overspill pipe. The dagger flew out of his hand and he barely had time to scream before his head was sucked under and his feet flew up into the air, as he somersaulted and was sucked under the water.

I didn't even stop to think. I reached out to the dagger and caught it, letting go of Raven as I shouted, 'Deal with him, Toby!' and threw Toby the Diamond Dagger. He was the only one near enough to strike Raven with it. I'd blown his cover, that was certain – but I just had to hope he could kill Raven and get control of the Kataki without me.

As a police helicopter searchlight illuminated the water, I threw myself into the reservoir. But the water was a million times more powerful than me, and I was immediately sucked into the overflow pipe, tumbling over and over like I was in a washing machine. Luckily, the water level had dropped enough that it was more like an industrial water-slide, but even so, the water was turbulent as I tried to keep my head high enough to grab some much-needed air. I was swept so fast down the pipe, the air was knocked out of me again.

How could I be so stupid! Letting Mr Bell attack Mad Dog. I couldn't bear life without him! I took one last gulp as I bobbed back up, then I held on to the breath, just hoping that Mad Dog had been able to do the same. I had no idea how long it would take to get to the other end of this pipe, but I was destined never to find out because suddenly the water whooshed to one side, carrying me into the castle cellar. The overspill pipe had been blocked off, diverting the course of the water into Raven's storage area. My mind flashed to the hang-glider who'd dropped the bomb into the reservoir, and I hoped it had been Yazuki and that this was all part of her mission – to flood the castle and destroy all Raven's explosives and supplies.

I pulled myself to my feet, trying not to make too much noise as I coughed and spluttered to clear my lungs. There was no time to stop and think. The cellar was waist-high in water. I waded along, feeling everywhere with my hands and feet, looking for any sign of Mad Dog. I made my way as fast as I could, wanting to shout, but knowing there were Kataki right above me. They'd all flown back here with their unexploded bombs and I could hear the panic as they ran about trying to salvage things and escape before the police turned up.

I made my way towards Ridley's empty cell. The door was open with the key in it. I saw something moving – just a tiny shadow at first, then a small furry body appeared.

'Bushi!' I whispered, as my precious rat made her way across the bars of the cell towards me. She was wet and shivering and, as I looked closer, I could see the string on the key to the cell door had been gnawed. 'You rescued Ridley?'

She answered with the tiniest squeak, which wasn't anything to do with my question. She was trying to tell me something else as she jumped into the water and started swimming.

'Is it Akira?' I called softly. 'Where is he?' But it wasn't Akira she was leading me to. Up ahead, the coffin with my name on had been washed up against the end cell. I paused, relieved that I'd stopped the dam being blown up without ending up dead in that awful box. But as Bushi led me nearer to it, I saw something that was nearly as bad. My stomach lurched.

Another body, limp and lifeless, was face down inside the rough wooden coffin.

'Mad Dog!' I gasped, wading towards him to feel the pulse on his neck. He was breathing, but only just. I had to get him out of here, away from danger, to find out how badly he was hurt and what help he needed.

I could hear sirens everywhere in the distance now, along with the Kataki rushing round even more frantically above me. I had no idea how to get Mad Dog out, but help was nearer than I realised. Ridley may have gone, but someone else was down here with me. At first I was afraid it was Raven or Mr Bell – but a kind voice with a Yorkshire accent called softly, 'I'm here, Hattie, let me help!'

I knew straight away it must be the guard who had helped Ridley send the postcard to me. I had to trust him – I had no choice. Mad Dog's life could depend on it. I pushed the floating coffin along the dungeon corridor to meet him as Bushi climbed on to my shoulder, then down into the safety of my top pocket.

'We'll get him round to the back steps but then we'll have to carry him,' the man whispered.

'Where's Ridley?'

The guard shook his head. 'Seems he let himself out somehow. At least I hope he did. Must have had help – don't know how he got the key.'

I didn't waste time explaining about Bushi. Together we

pushed on through the flooded dungeon, looking at all the floating debris – all Raven's explosives and emergency services clothes, his vans, everything destroyed. My eyes scanned every centimetre for Akira, but he was nowhere to be seen. I even whistled softly for him. I desperately wanted to stop and look for him, though I didn't even know if he was still alive. I wanted to search for Ridley as well, to make sure he was safe. But Mad Dog needed me, so I waded on through the water as fast as my legs would take me.

As we got to the stairs leading up to the ground floor, there was more help at hand. The friendly guard ran ahead up the stone steps and opened the big, wooden door. Yazuki was already there – and Mum, Toby, Neena and Takumi, all of them still looking exactly like me. I knew this was so that if anyone caught us, they'd have trouble telling which one was the real Hattori Hachi. The confusion could give us a few precious moments that could still help save my life. They all helped lift Mad Dog out of the wooden box, except Toby who was still guarding the Diamond Dagger, trying to keep it hidden under his ninja jacket.

In minutes, Dad was at the castle with our car – but not before the rest of Raven's army arrived, fleeing the reservoir. They were getting closer by the second as the police sirens got louder. The helicopter approached overhead, shining its light on the castle. We could hear the Kataki making their way down into the dungeon as we silently carried Mad Dog up the steps and out through the castle's back door. Suddenly one of them shouted, 'She's there! There's loads of them!'

We raced to get Mad Dog into the car and we all climbed in after him. Kataki were coming from all directions as Dad started the engine.

'Thank you,' I whispered to the guard, 'whoever you are.'

'Al,' he whispered as he turned away and he and Takumi went off to try and stop the Kataki from following us.

CHAPTER FOURTEEN

'Born a ninja, live a ninja, die a ninja!'

With no traffic on the roads, it was a four and a half hour drive home. Dad was bursting with questions for Mum. 'What have you been up to? How long have you been involved with all this ninjutsu? Is it true that . . .' He trailed off and I knew that most of all, he wanted to ask her about Toby.

'We'll talk about everything when we get home,' was her reply. We were crammed in – Mum and Dad in the front, me and Yazuki on either side of Toby in the back and Neena squeezed in amongst our bags, watching over Mad Dog in the hatchback. He was drifting in and out of consciousness. I wished we could get him checked out at a hospital, but I knew we had to get the Diamond Dagger home and stored somewhere safe. Dad had wrapped it in an old car blanket and put it under his seat where we couldn't be tempted to get it out and look at it.

With none of us wanting to talk until Mum had answered some of Dad's questions, we drove home in almost total silence. I was the only one to speak, to ask Toby, 'Did you kill Raven?'

Mum answered for him. 'He didn't have a chance. The police helicopter flew in and everyone fled.'

'He got away?'

'As I said, we'll talk once we're home,' Mum said.

I held Bushi all the way back. She twitched her whiskers and didn't sleep at all. We pulled up outside our house as dawn was breaking. We all piled out and Dad and Toby carried Mad Dog upstairs while Mum parked the car and made sure we were all safely locked indoors. Yazuki ran down to the dojo to make some calls and try and find out what we should do next. We put Mad Dog in my bed and Neena brought herbal medicine and poultices up from the dojo and she and I sat with him while Mum and Dad disappeared into their bedroom for an intense discussion. I was worried sick and felt guilty that I hadn't saved Mad Dog from Mr Bell.

Eventually, I went into the living room to see if Toby was okay. He was just sitting on the sofa with his head in his hands. Before I could say anything, Dad emerged from his bedroom. I was sort of relieved Mad Dog wasn't able to witness what happened next. I knew he couldn't have helped but feel envious, because Mad Dog so badly wanted a father himself. Toby got up and he and Dad just stood for what seemed like an age, looking at each other, standing man to man.

Eventually, Dad simply said, 'I'm proud and honoured that you're my son.'

I think it took Toby by surprise – maybe he was expecting trouble for having been so rough on us all at the castle. He just stood there nodding, like he wanted to speak but couldn't because he was so choked. Then he half whispered, 'I'm pretty screwed up, Dad.'

Dad took him in his arms and held him.

Now I was the one crying. Well, me and Mum as she came back into the living room. And Neena as well, as she peered out from my bedroom to see what was going on.

For me, it was as though my life had finally joined back together. That's the only way I can describe it. Something had been missing all these years and I'd never known what. I was an only child but I didn't feel like it. And through all this misery and confusion and ninja deception, deep down I'd still always believed Toby would come home. He broke away from Dad and turned to me. We didn't need to hug or anything. I just smiled and he did too, and in unison we both said, 'You okay?' Then, 'Yes thanks.' Then, 'Me too.' Our eyes locked and, for a second, I thought my brain would explode as images from Toby's life flashed into my mind. I had finally managed to mind-merge with him, but there was just too much to take in.

Toby jumped back, startled, and said, 'Later, maybe?'

'Yes, we've got hours, weeks – the rest of our lives to catch up,' I replied.

Mum quickly filled us in on what had happened over the

last few days. Even before they'd left home, she and Yazuki had received orders from two different *chunin*. Mum had been told to keep hold of the scroll, so she'd got Yazuki to take it from the dojo safe and make it look as though it had been stolen so no one would suspect they had it. Mad Dog and I had disturbed Yazuki, but she couldn't let us know what she was up to, in case the enemy tried to torture the information out of us. Once in Kielder, Mum and Yazuki had separated. Their *chunin* had each made plans for them to infiltrate Raven's training camp, but once inside they'd never spoken to each other, truly understanding – and trusting – that they must only do as instructed, and not jeopardise the mission.

Yazuki had been told to destroy the enemy camp – and any weapons, which she'd discovered included kilos of explosives. She'd carried out her mission magnificently by blowing up the sluice gate to the overflow pipe, having made sure the door from the tunnel into the dungeons was jammed open, causing all the flood water to gush into the castle and destroy just about everything.

Mum's task had been really clear: *Make Toby the Golden Child*. She hadn't been told why, but had guessed this was so Toby could carry on pretending to be one of the Kataki. This would mean Raven wouldn't need to kill me with the Diamond Dagger, and my life would no longer be in danger. Toby confirmed this. When he fled the Foundry, after we rescued Mum, he'd wanted to come and be part of our family. But he'd already pledged allegiance to Raven and their bond was so strong that Toby had been contacted by someone high up in the Hattori family who had told him that he was more useful on the inside and ordered him to stay until Raven and the Kataki could be successfully defeated. So Toby stayed on, bravely playing the villain, while we were all put in place to carry out our *jonin*'s plan.

'I don't understand,' I said. 'Why was I even called to Kielder in the first place?'

'It was Ridley,' Toby replied. 'No one could find the dagger and he knew your presence would bring it out of its hiding place. And it did.'

'Thanks to Dad,' I said. 'He solved Great-granddad Jacko's cryptic postcard that made the connection to the bell tower.'

'Yes, but you brought him to Kielder in the first place – and it was you who found the Diamond Dagger,' said Yazuki. 'Without you, Raven would have carried out his plan and hundreds of people would have died last night. Give yourself credit for that at least, Hattie.'

Right now, I didn't want to give myself credit for anything. I felt far too dreadful about Mad Dog. Miserably, I looked for every other mistake I'd made at the reservoir.

'I wasn't supposed to sign the scroll,' I said. 'If I'd thought about it, I'd have realised what was going on. But that dagger . . .'

'Yes, it has a life of its own,' Toby said. 'It really is a dangerous piece of metal.'

'Everyone wanted Toby to be the Golden Child,' I sighed, feeling a real pang of guilt. 'I'm sorry, Toby – I never

219

meant to take that away from you.'

'I'm sure we'll discover it was just a stop-gap plan,' Mum quickly reassured me, 'and not a great one, to be honest – because it would have given Raven access to all the Hattoris' land and wealth and everything beyond, and he'd have wanted it straightaway. Who knows if our *jonin* even had a plan for how we were going to get Toby out of there.'

'Yes,' Toby continued. 'It was only supposed to buy some time for us all to work out a plan to defeat Raven, without the panic of our sixteenth birthdays looming. And anyway, it's a good thing – and proper – that you signed.' He glanced at Mum.

'We believe there's a bigger prophecy, Hattie,' Mum explained in her gentle reassuring voice that I knew meant there was more big news to come. 'A prophecy that involves a Golden Child who is still pure.'

My heart leapt – my mind raced to the kissing I'd done with Mad Dog at the Foundry and all the feelings I'd had for him since. I desperately hoped this hadn't sullied me somehow for what was about to follow. But I needn't have worried.

'A pure Golden Child is one who has not killed anybody,' Yazuki explained. 'I trust that's still the case?'

I exhaled. 'Yes, no, I mean yes it is the case, I haven't killed anyone, so no worries there,' I said.

'We believe it was your destiny to become the Golden Child,' Yazuki continued.

That triggered a memory. 'Yes, I felt this voice inside me – telling me to sign because it was my destiny,' I said. 'I don't know if it was me telling myself that . . .'

Yazuki nodded. 'More likely a mind-connection far more important than you can know right now,' she said. 'The time will come when you will use your status to halt the endless years of feuding and fighting. It is as it is and you must not fret.'

'Another pretty weird birthday, then, Hattie,' said Neena, still standing in the doorway of my bedroom. 'By the way, happy birthday Toby as well. Sorry, but I didn't get either of you a card. I was going to shop this weekend but time kind of ran away with me.'

A faint voice called from my bedroom. 'Yes, happy birthday, you two!' I ran in to see Mad Dog sitting up in bed, looking a thousand times better. He had a bowl of water and a flannel and was wiping his face with one hand and cleaning his teeth with my toothbrush with the other.

'Welcome back,' I said, putting Bushi into her golden temple cage.

'Happy birthday,' he said. 'Sweet sixteen.'

Neena straightened out the bed, gave Mad Dog a glass of water, then said, 'I'll leave you two to it.' She went out and shut the door. Mad Dog rinsed out his mouth, then looked at me. The two of us just stared at each other for a moment.

'I had no choice,' I said. 'I knew Toby was on our side and I thought you were going to kill him.'

'It's okay.' He smiled, but I was afraid something had changed between us forever. I'd let Mr Bell attack him – he could have killed him and I didn't try to stop him and we both knew it.

'It's sucks sometimes, this ninjutsu,' Mad Dog eventually said, patting the bed.

I sank down beside him. I felt unusually defeated. 'I love you, Mad Dog. I'd give my life for you – but I just couldn't let you kill Toby.'

'I know, I know, I know,' he said. 'Listen, it was my fault as much as anyone.'

'You didn't know! You were just trying to protect me.'

'I did know – if I'd really thought about it. I kidded myself I could be the big hero because your dad wasn't stepping in to help you – but your mum wasn't either, nor Yazuki. I knew deep down Toby wasn't a threat, but somehow I couldn't stop myself and I screwed up everything.'

'Not as much as I did,' I said. 'Toby was supposed to sign the scroll.'

'No he wasn't – not really. Not for the long-term good. I heard what they said to you just now. There's a bigger destiny for you, Hattie. And I want to be the one by your side, helping you achieve it.'

I sighed heavily. I was so tired and so upset by everything that had happened in Kielder, I just couldn't think straight.

'Want your birthday present?' he said.

I nodded.

Mad Dog kissed me – just a peck on my forehead. He hugged me and a sense of calm engulfed me. He was warm and smelt of soap and toothpaste and for a moment I was no longer worried or anxious. I felt him put something round my neck. He did up a clasp, then sat back. I looked down and there was the sweetest little necklace. Two rats, made of silver, curled up with each other.

'Got it made specially,' he said.

'Thanks,' I replied, but my voice was already cracking. 'It's lovely, but —'

'You didn't find Akira then?'

I shook my head. 'We had to leave . . .' I trailed off, not able to bear it. 'Guess I'll never know what happened.'

'We can't have that – it's too sad,' Mad Dog said. With that, a tiny nose appeared from under my duvet, whiskers twitching.

'Akira!' I squealed, as my beautiful rat ran towards me and climbed straight on to my shoulder. Bushi shot out of her cage, which I never kept locked, and ran across the floor, up the duvet and straight up my back to join him. They were happy as anything to see each other, sniffing each other's faces and twitching whiskers. 'Where was he?!'

'In the castle dungeons. Keeping watch over Ridley. I was still conscious when the flood water spewed me into the cellar but I passed out pretty quickly. The last thing I saw was these two beauties carrying a key to Ridley so he could escape. They must have chewed through one of the guard's belts. When I woke up just now Akira was in my pocket,' said Mad Dog, pulling out his leather pouch where Akira always slept. 'He must have stayed with me to look after me. I didn't even crush him,' he boasted, beaming.

Mad Dog mentioning Ridley made me feel upset all over again. 'You didn't see what happened to Ridley?'

Mad Dog shook his head, then took my hand and squeezed it.

'Thanks for the lovely necklace,' I said. 'And for getting Akira home safely.'

He hugged me, then said in his teasing voice, 'Tell me that bit about how you love me again . . .'

Dad broke the moment, shouting from the living room, 'Why don't you two come through? Yazuki's got some news.'

In the living room, Yazuki was now in her laundry overalls, looking every bit the fit and energetic fifty-two-year-old niece of old Yazuki, Kuyu – who she pretended to be whenever she was in Camden. She was pouring hot water into her best Japanese teapot. She smiled happily as I came into the living room, followed by Mad Dog, wrapped in my duvet. She put the lid on the pot and placed it on the coffee table, which she'd set with our flourishing bonsai tree, two candles and a small Buddha she must have brought up from the dojo. She'd spread cushions around the floor for us all to sit on. The Diamond Dagger was the centrepiece, diamonds twinkling, though not quite as bright as I remembered them at the reservoir, perhaps because the dagger wasn't in action now, about to fight or kill someone.

'No one touches that dagger without my say-so,' said Dad, sitting next to Mum. Toby placed himself at the head of the table while Yazuki sat on his left and Mad Dog and I squeezed in on his right.

'Firstly,' Yazuki said, in her soft, ceremonial voice, 'I want to welcome Toby properly into the Jackson family.

Neena hesitated, looking awkward. 'Maybe I should go, if it's a family thing.'

'Not at all, Neena,' said Yazuki. 'You belong in this circle as much as I do. Come and join us.'

Toby moved up and Neena squeezed in next to him. She blushed very slightly and I remembered how much she'd fancied him the first time they'd met all those months ago.

Yazuki poured seven cups of tea. She put down the teapot and looked each of us in the eye before speaking.

'There are rumours that there are three Diamond Daggers, that together make up the most important legend in ninjutsu history,' she said.

'Do they all have the same killing power over a Golden Child?' I asked.

'I don't know,' she answered. 'Nearly a thousand years ago, the three Diamond Daggers were gifted one to each of a powerful Emperor's three children. His name was Emperor Mikito and he was an ancestor of the Hattori family. This family, currently ending with Toby and Hattie, is the line that descended from the eldest of those three children. The daggers represent the three sacred symbols of sovereign rule – mirror, stone and magatman, which is a beautiful, oriental bead, shaped like a cashew nut, that represents harmony. When touched, each dagger emits a beautiful sound and it is said in legend that, when in battle, they remember every harsh act that has gone before and take on a life of their own. Only when all three are together, can the sum of the information on each of the handles be understood. Together, they lead to great power, wealth – and a secret location.' We all stared at the squiggles and Japanese characters etched into the handle.

'Do you know what any of those words say?' I asked.

'They are written in very old script, so no,' Yazuki answered. 'This is all I know – except that it's believed the secret location is near the Hattori family home on the island of Kyushu in Japan. There has been no word from our *jonin* or my *chunin*, so for now we carry on as usual. Hattie, you will sit your GCSE exams, resuming on Friday and, Toby, we will now start the official process of "adopting" you into the Jackson family. This will be the easiest way to explain our new situation here.'

'Okay,' said Toby. I felt Mad Dog bristle, so I took his hand under the table and gave it a squeeze. It was so hard for him, seeing my family expanding when he didn't have one of his own.

'Any questions?' Yazuki said, then took a sip of tea while she waited.

'So we have no idea where Raven is or what his next plan might be,' Mum said, stating the obvious.

'Just that he's now homeless, furious, shamed in front of his army and without the Diamond Dagger, the scroll or Toby or Hattie,' Yazuki said. She couldn't help smiling.

'I think we can call that quite a success on our part,' Dad said.

'Was no one captured up at Kielder?' Neena asked. 'What do they think happened to cause the explosion?'

'That was a very smart cover up by the Kataki,' Yazuki

226

said. 'Very quick thinking on their part. A news report on the radio just announced that a rogue bomb was misfired from the army range at Otterburn and landed in the reservoir. Timely proof that the Kataki really do have infiltrators in extremely high places. It's believed no damage was done other than flooding the castle – and, by the time the authorities got access, apparently there was nothing at all inside the castle walls. No dojo or anything. By the sound of things, it was as though the Kataki just evaporated, disappearing with everything as secretly as they arrived.'

Dad raised his teacup. 'Well, I'd like to propose a toast,' he said. 'To Hattori Hachi – our quick-thinking, multi-talented Golden Child!'

'Hattori Hachi!' everyone said, raising their teacups as well.

'I just wish I knew who our *jonin* is,' I said. 'There's so much I want to find out.'

Our ceremony was interrupted by a loud ring, as the downstairs doorbell sent the videophone into action. Tasha Weaver was there, practically bursting.

'What does she want?' I said, groaning and getting to my feet.

'Toby, most likely,' Neena mumbled, giving Toby her sweetest grin.

I pressed the intercom. 'Hi Tasha!' I said. 'I'm just tied up at the moment, but can I —'

'Happy Birthday!' she shrieked, cutting me off. 'Brought your birthday pizza – let me in, just a sec. I've got some unbelievable news!'

'How does she know it's my birthday?' I said.

'That was me,' said Mad Dog. 'When I picked up the pizzas the other day, I arranged a birthday surprise.'

Everyone started rushing round, clearing away the dagger and the tea ceremony while Mad Dog went to put on some clothes and Toby hid in Mum and Dad's bedroom. I waited a second, then pressed the buzzer to open the front door.

'Make sure to shut the door behind you!' I said. But before the words had left my lips, I saw two people on the videophone following Tasha in. One was her mum, Sheila, but the other looked like a man. Dad took the dagger back out from where he was hiding it under the kitchen sink and kept it in his hands but out of sight, shielded by the breakfast bar that jutted out into our living room. Mum glanced at Yazuki as she took a protective umbrella from the stand. Yazuki moved next to the heavy Buddha statue that could act as a weapon if she needed to grab it to fight someone.

Tasha arrived at the top of the stairs and knocked on our apartment door. I opened it, very cautiously. She didn't even wait for me to say, 'Hi, come in,' she just burst in, carrying four large pizza boxes and said, 'It's a miracle! You'll never believe it – Dad's home!'

Sheila followed her in, tearful and thrilled. 'You'll never guess what happened!' she blurted. 'He had an accident four years ago, lost his memory. Been living in a home – but then he had a fall and he remembered who he was again. He's back! Come on, Al – come on in!'

A man walked into the room. None of us spoke. Eventually he smiled and in a soft, East Yorkshire accent, he said, 'It's good to be back. It's a long while since I've felt normal.'

There was no mistaking that face. It was Al, our guard from the castle.

Yazuki said in her matter-of-fact, soft Japanese Kuyu voice, 'We are all most pleased to meet you, Al. Welcome to Jackson home. Very special people, Jacksons.'

'So I've heard,' he said, coming over to shake our hands, each in turn.

'Nasty gash on your head,' I said.

'Other guys all came off worse.' He smiled. 'They won't be bothering anyone for a while.'

'He's teasing,' Sheila said. 'Al's never fought anyone in his life!'

'Actually, I did this time,' he said. 'I helped a blind man who had escaped from a prison cell, but couldn't find his way to safety – some bad people were attacking him so a friend and I made sure he got away safely.' My heart leapt. I knew he was telling me in code what I was desperate to hear about Ridley. Sheila just laughed uproariously.

'Yes, and I wonder what other tall stories that knock on the head has given you!'

Tasha opened up the four boxes. Each pizza had *Happy Birthday, Hattie* written in melted cheese.

'Present from Mad Dog!' Tasha grinned, like she was Cupid or something.

Mad Dog appeared from my bedroom, dressed in some of my sweat pants and my T-shirt with a red heart on it. Tasha raised an eyebrow and looked at me, smirking.

'Pepperoni – my favourite,' I said. 'Thanks, Mad Dog.'

He smiled at me and my heart skipped a beat all over again.

When Toby stepped out of Mum and Dad's bedroom, Tasha nearly fainted. Pure joy welled up on her face as she looked at him, then at her dad, and cried out in a very dramatic, Tasha-like way, 'My life is now completely perfect!' She ran over and hugged him, crying. He was pretty manly and cool about seeing her – but actually, I could tell he was enjoying it. Neena and I exchanged looks. Tasha Weaver back in our lives again – great . . . But if she really was Al's daughter, then there was obviously more to all this than met the eye. For now I wasn't going to worry. I was delighted, in fact, that the wonderful Al was going to be over the street, no doubt keeping an eye on us all.

'So what's new?' Toby said.

'Quite a lot,' Sheila replied. 'Our street's been twinned with a lovely village in Japan. They approached me out of the blue. I'm arranging an ambassadorial trip this summer. I hope you'll all come?'

'Where is it?' Neena asked.

'Okinato,' said Sheila. 'On the island of Kyushu. Near Nagasaki – though of course it's not the decimated place it was just after the atomic bomb. I hear it's very beautiful these days.'

'That's where you grew up, isn't it Mum?' I said.

'What a coincidence,' she replied – though we both knew it wasn't likely to be coincidental at all.

'We'll all be ready for a trip to Japan by this summer,'

Mad Dog said, smiling. 'I hear there's loads to do out there. Always wanted to go to Japan, haven't you, Hattie?'

'Yes, I'd love to,' was all I could think to answer.

'And me,' said Toby.

'Us too,' said Dad, taking Mum's hand. 'And Kuyu, you'd probably fancy a trip back home to visit our twin town, wouldn't you?'

'Most certainly,' she answered. 'Perhaps we can invite Yazuki.'

'That would be very interesting indeed,' I said, wondering how Kuyu and Yazuki could be in one place at the same time.

Neena piped up last. 'Never a dull moment in this household,' she said. 'Put my name down as well, if that's okay with you, Hattie?'

I smiled, feeling happier and safer now as I looked round at all these supportive faces.

'Of course, Neena. Wouldn't dream of going anywhere without you,' I said, knowing that if we went to Japan I'd need all the help I could get, because not one, but two deadly enemies – Praying Mantis and Raven – would probably be waiting for me there.

Special Thanks

So many people have helped Hattori Hachi on her way since book one was published, and I owe thanks to them all.
To Brenda, Ruth, Melissa and everyone at Piccadilly Press who have launched Hattie Jackson into the world with such style and hard work.
Thanks too to all the reviewers who have been so enthusiastic, especially Moira Briggs, Jay Benedict and Edna Hobbs and the young voices – Alfie Keenan, Bella Wickens, Francesca and Hugo Forte, Claire Mitchell and Jack Davis.
My family have been as fab as ever, and I owe special thanks to Helen Prowse for her help in promoting the books.
A huge thank you to Ian and Ben for taking me on such an inspirational trip to Kielder; to our ninja cats, Mitten and Buffy, who have purred throughout and made me take time out to think things through; Rochelle Stevens for her constant encouragement and attention to detail; Jaqueline Danson for doing such a terrific job on the new website; and all my friends who cheer me on whenever I'm flagging.
The biggest thanks of all goes to you, the readers, who have sent great feedback via the website and enthused me to write book two and now book three as well. Thank you!

Discover the world of Hattori Hachi!

Join me online for more about my life and what's coming next.
You can even write a review or choose your own animus!

www.hattorihachi.com